Alphonse Daudet

In the Midst of Paris

Alphonse Daudet

In the Midst of Paris

ISBN/EAN: 9783337084882

Printed in Europe, USA, Canada, Australia, Japan

Cover: Foto ©Andreas Hilbeck / pixelio.de

More available books at **www.hansebooks.com**

In the Midst of

PARIS

By ALPHONSE DAUDET

TRANSLATED BY
CÉLINE BERTAULT

NEW YORK
PLATT, BRUCE & COMPANY
70 FIFTH AVENUE
1896

THE LAFAYETTE PRESS, NEW YORK.

CONTENTS.

LIST OF ILLUSTRATIONS.

IN THE MIDST OF

PARIS

CHAPTER I.

THE SIEGE.

E were returning up the avenue of the Champs Elysées with Doctor V., asking him about the walls riddled with shells, the pavements torn up by grape-shot, in fact, the history of the Siege of Paris, when, just before we got to the Place de l'Etoile, the doctor stopped, and pointing out one of those handsome corner houses grouped around the Arc de Triomphe, said :—

13

" Do you see those four closed windows up there, over the balcony ?

" In the early days of the month of August—that terrible August of the year '70—so charged with storms and disasters, I was called in there to a frightful case of apoplexy. It was to Colonel Jouve, a cuirassier of the First Empire, an old man infatuated with patriotic pride who, at the commencement of the war, had come to lodge in the Champs Elysées, in a balcony apartment. Guess why ! To be present at the triumphant return of our troops ! Poor old man ! The news of Wissembourg came to him as he was rising from table. On reading the name of Napoleon at the foot of that bulletin of defeat, he fell thunderstruck.

" I found the old cuirassier stretched at full length on the carpet, his face bloody and lifeless, as if he had been struck a blow on the head with a club.

"Standing, he must have been very tall; lying, he looked immense. With beautiful features, superb teeth, and a fine head of curly white hair, though he was nearly eighty, he looked like sixty years old. Near him, on her knees, was his granddaughter. She so resembled him that, seeing them side by side, you would have been reminded of two beautiful Greek medals struck from the same stamp; only the one was old, dull, and rather indistinct in the outlines; the other was resplendent and clean cut, with all the brilliancy and smoothness of a new impression.

"The grief of this child touched me. Daughter and granddaughter of soldiers, her father was at Mac-Mahon's headquarters, and the sight of this grand old man stretched before her brought another no less terrible image to her mind.

"I endeavored to reassure her, but, in reality, I had little hope. We had to deal with a severe case of hemiplegy, and recovery was scarcely to be hoped for at eighty. For three days the patient remained in the same state of motionless stupor. In the midst of all this the news of Reischoffen arrived in Paris. You remember in what a strange fashion. Until evening we all believed in a great victory, 20,000 Prussians killed, and the Crown Prince a prisoner!

"I know not by what miracle, or by what magnetic current, an echo of the national joy penetrated to our poor deaf-mute, even to his paralyzed limbs; certain it is that, on approaching his bed that evening, I found him

a different man. His eye was almost
clear, his tongue less stiff. He had
strength to smile, and to stammer
twice, 'Vic-to-ry!'

" 'Yes, Colonel, a grand victory!'

" And as I gave him details of
MacMahon's brilliant success, I saw
his features relax and his face light
up. When I went out, the young
girl was waiting for me, standing
pale and sobbing at the door.

" 'But he is saved!' said I, taking
her hands.

" The unhappy child had scarcely
courage to answer me. They had
just posted up the true version of
Reischoffen — MacMahon put to
flight, the whole army crushed. We
looked at each other in consternation.
She was distressed in thinking of her
father.

" I trembled for the old man. It

2

was very certain he could not resist
this new shock. And yet, what
could we do? Leave him his joy—
the illusions which had called him
back to life? But then it would be
necessary to lie!

" 'Very well, then, I shall lie,'
said the heroic girl, quickly drying
her tears, and she returned radiant to
her grandfather's room.

" She had set herself a hard task.
The first few days were got through
without much difficulty. The good
man's head was weak, and he allowed
himself to be deceived like a child.
But with returning health, his ideas
became clearer.

" We had to keep him acquainted
with the movements of the armies
and to draw up for him military
bulletins. It was a sad pity to see
that beautiful girl, night and day,

over her maps of Germany, marking
out the battles with little flags, and
trying to invent a glorious campaign :
Bazaine descending upon Berlin,
Frossard in Bavaria, MacMahon on
the Baltic. For all this she asked
my advice, and I helped her as much
as I could, but it was the grandfather himself who served us best
in this imaginary invasion. He had
conquered Germany so often under
the First Empire ! He knew all the
moves beforehand: 'See, now they
will go there, they will do that,' and
his forecasts were always realized,
which did not fail to make him very
proud.

"Unfortunately it was in vain that
we took towns and gained battles ; we
never went fast enough for that insati-
able old fellow ! Every day,when I
arrived, I heard of a new feat of arms.

"'Doctor, we have taken Mayence,' the young girl told me, coming towards me with a heart-breaking smile, and I heard, through the door, a delighted voice crying:—

"'We're getting on! We're getting on! . . . In a week we shall enter Berlin!'

"At that moment the Prussians were not more than a week from Paris. . . . We asked ourselves at first whether it would not be better to remove him into the country; but, once outside, the state of France would have revealed everything to him, and I thought him still too weak, and too much stunned by the great shock he had already received, to know the truth. It was decided, therefore, to let him remain.

"On the first day that Paris was invested, I went up to their house, I remember, much moved with the anguish of heart that the closing of all the gates of Paris, the battle under the walls, and the changing of our villages into frontiers brought us. I found the old gentleman jubilant and proud.

" ' Well,' said he, ' here is the siege begun ! '

" I looked at him in astonishment.

" ' What, Colonel, do you know ——— ? '

" His granddaughter turned to me :——

" ' Ah ! yes, Doctor. That is the great news. The Siege of Berlin has commenced.'

" This she said, drawing out her needle with such a staid little air, and so tranquilly—how could he suspect anything ?

"The cannon from the forts! He could not hear them. This poor Paris, wretched and convulsed! He could not see it.

"What he *could* see from his bed was a bit of the Arc de Triomphe, and in his room was a whole curiosity shop of the First Empire, well calculated to maintain his illusions. Portraits of Marshals, engravings of battles, the King of Rome in a baby's robe; then large stiff consoles, ornamented with copper trophies, laden with Imperial relics, medals, bronzes, a stone from St. Helena, under a shade, miniatures—all representing the same lady, becurled, in ball costume, in a yellow dress with leg-of-mutton sleeves, and bright eyes—it was all this, the atmosphere of victories and conquests, much more than anything we could tell him, that made the brave Colonel believe so naïvely in the Siege of Berlin.

" From that day our military operations were very much simplified. To take Berlin was now only an affair of patience.

" From time to time, when the old man became too impatient, a letter was read to him from his son—an imaginary letter, of course, since nothing could now get into Paris, and because, since Sedan, Mac-Mahon's aide-de-camp had been drafted off to a German fortress. Imagine the despair of that poor child, without news of her father, knowing him a prisoner, deprived of every comfort, perhaps ill, and yet obliged to make him speak in those cheerful letters—they were rather short letters, as might be expected from a soldier in the field—of advancing steadily into the conquered country.

"Sometimes strength failed her, and, consequently, there were weeks without any news. But the old man got uneasy, and could not sleep. Then promptly came a letter from Germany, which she brought and read gayly to him at his bedside, keeping back her tears. The Colónel listened religiously, smiled with an intelligent air, approved, criticised, and explained to us the difficult passages. But where he was especially fine was in the answers he sent to his son : 'Never forget that you are a Frenchman,' said he. 'Be generous to those poor people. Do not make the invasion too heavy for them.' And then there were endless recommendations, adorable twaddle about respect

for the proprieties, the politeness
due to ladies—in fact, a complete
code of military honor for the use of
conquerors! He added also some
general observations on politics, and
the conditions to be imposed on the
conquered. On that point, I must
say, he was not unreasonable.

" 'A war indemnity, and nothing
further. What is the good of taking
their provinces? Can you make
France out of Germany?'

" He dictated all this with a firm
voice, and one felt there was so
much candor in his words, such
a fine, patriotic faith, that it was
impossible to listen to him unmoved.

"All this time the siege was advancing—not that of Berlin, alas!
It was a time of great cold, bom-
bardments, epidemics, and famine.

But, thanks to our care, our efforts, and the indefatigable tenderness which surrounded him, the serenity of the old man was never for an instant disturbed. Up to the end, I was able to get him white bread and fresh meat.

"There was only enough for him, and you can imagine nothing more touching than those breakfasts of the grandfather, so innocently selfish—the old man upon his bed, fresh and smiling, his serviette tucked under his chin; near him his granddaughter, a little pale from her privations, guiding his hands, giving him drink, helping him to all those forbidden good things. Then, revived by the repast, in the comfort of his warm room, with the winter wind outside, and the snow whirling past his windows, the old cuirassier recalled his

campaigns in the north, and related
to us for the hundredth time that sad
retreat from Russia, in which they
had nothing to eat but frozen biscuit
and horse-flesh.

"'Do you understand, little one?
We used to eat horses.'

"She understood only too well.
For two months she had eaten nothing else. From day to day, however,
as convalescence progressed, our task
beside the invalid became more difficult. That paralysis of his senses, .
and of all his limbs, which had served
us so well up to this time, began
to disappear. Two or three times
already the terrible volleys from the
Maillot Gate had made him start,
and prick up his ears like a grey-
hound; we were obliged to invent a
last victory for Bazaine, under Berlin, and salvos fired in his honor at

the Invalides. Another day his bed had been moved to the window—it was, I believe, the Thursday of Rezonville—and he saw the National Guards massed together on the Avenue of the Grande Armée.

" 'What are those troops doing there?' he demanded; and we heard him mutter between his teeth: ' Bad form! bad form !'

" Nothing else happened; but we understood that, in future, we must take great precautions. Unhappily, we were not cautious enough.

" One evening when I arrived the child came to me full of trouble.

" ·It is to-morrow they enter,' she said.

" Was the grandfather's door open ? The fact is, that in thinking over it afterwards, I remembered that his face had, on that evening, an extraordinary expression. It is probable that he heard us.

"Only *we* spoke of the Prussians, while *he* thought of the French, in that triumphal entry which he had so long expected—MacMahon coming down the avenue in the midst of flowers and the flourish of trumpets, his son beside the Marshal, and he, the old father, upon his balcony, in full uniform, as at Lutzen, saluting the torn flags and the eagles blackened with powder.

"Poor father Jouve! He doubtless fancied that we wished to prevent him from being present at this march-past of the troops to avoid too great an excitement for him.

"He took care to speak to no one; but the next day, at the very hour in which the Prussians were timidly entering on the long road leading from the Maillot Gate to the Tuileries, the window just above there opened softly, and the Colonel appeared on the balcony, with his helmet, his big cavalry sword, and all the glorious equipment of a Milhaud cuirassier.

"I still ask myself what effort of will, what fresh spring of life, could have thus placed him again on his feet, and in harness! Be that as it may, there he was, standing behind the railing, wondering to find the avenues so wide, so silent; the shutters of the houses closed; Paris dismal as a lazaretto; flags everywhere, but so strange, all white with red crosses, and no crowd running before our soldiers.

"For a moment, he may possibly have thought he was mistaken——

"But, no! Yonder, behind the Arc de Triomphe, was a confused noise, a black line advancing in the growing daylight. . . . Then, gradually, the peaks of the helmets shone, the little drums of Jena began to beat, and under the Arc de l'Etoile, accompanied by the heavy rhythmic steps of the troops, and by the clash of sabres, burst forth Schubert's Triumphal March.

" Then, in the mournful silence of the place, rang out a cry, a terrible cry : ' To arms !—to arms !—the Prussians !' And the four Uhlans forming the advanced guard saw yonder on the balcony a tall, old man wave his arms, totter, and fall, rigid.

" This time Colonel Jouve was really dead."

CHAPTER II.

THE ENSIGN.

I.

HE regiment was engaged on the banks of a railway, and served as a target to the whole Prussian army massed in an opposite wood. They were firing on each other at a distance of eighty yards. The officers shouted, "Lie down!" but no one would obey, and the proud regiment remained standing, gathered round their colors.

In the great horizon of the setting sun, of cornfields, of pasture land, this confused group of men, enveloped in smoke, were like a flock of sheep surprised in the open country by the first whirlwind of a terrific storm.

It rained iron on that slope! nothing was heard but the crackle of the volleys and the prolonged vibration of the balls which flew from one end of the battle-field to the other. From time to time the flag, which waved overhead in the wind of the mitrailleuse, disappeared in the smoke, then a voice grave and steady, dominating the firing, the struggles of the dying, the oaths of the wounded, would cry: "*Au drapeau, mes enfants, au drapeau!*" Instantly an officer, vague as a shadow in the red mist, would spring forward, and the standard, once more alive as it were, showed again above the battle.

Twenty-two times it fell. Twenty-two times its staff, still warm, slipping

3

from a dying hand, was seized and upheld. and when, at sunset, what remained of the regiment—scarce a handful of men—retreated slowly, firing as they went. the colors were mere rags in the hands of Sergeant Hornus, the twenty-third ensign of the day.

II.

SERGEANT HORNUS was a crusty old war-dog, who could hardly write his own name. and who had taken twenty years to gain his sergeant's stripes. All the miseries of a foundling. all the brutalizing effects of barrack-life, could be traced in the low projecting forehead, the back bent beneath the knapsack, that air of careless self-neglect acquired in the ranks.

Besides all this he stammered. but then eloquence is not essential to an

ensign. On the evening of the battle his colonel said to him, " You have the colors, my brave fellow; keep them." And on his coarse hood, frayed by war and weather, the vivandière stitched the gold band of a sub-lieutenant.

This had been the one ambition of his humble life. From that moment he drew himself up; he who was wont to walk with bent head and eyes fixed on the ground, henceforth looked proudly upwards to the bit of stuff which he held very straight, high above death, treachery and defeat. Never was there a happier man than Hornus on days of battle, holding his staff firmly in its leather socket with both hands.

He neither spoke nor moved, and was as serious as a priest guarding some sacred thing. All his life,

all his strength, were concentrated
in the fingers grasping that gilded
rag upon which the balls beat so per-
sistently, and in his defiant eyes looking the Prussians full in the face, as
if saying, " Try, if you dare, to take
it from me ! "

No one did try, not even death.

After Borny, after Gravelotte,
those murderous battles, the colors
came out, tattered, in holes, transparent with wounds, but it was still
old Hornus who carried them.

III.

THEN came September with the
army around Metz, the investment,
and that long pause when the cannon
rusted in the mud, and the finest
troops in the world, demoralized by
inaction, want of food and want of

news. died of fever and *ennui* beside their piled arms. No one, neither chiefs nor soldiers, had faith in the future; Hornus alone was still confident. His ragged *tricolor* was all in all to him, and as long as he could see that, nothing seemed lost.

Unfortunately, as there was no more fighting, the colonel kept the colors at his house in one of the suburbs of Metz, and poor Hornus was much like a mother whose child is out to nurse. He thought of it constantly. Then when the yearning was too much for him, he went off to Metz, and, having seen it still in the same place, leaning against the wall, he returned full of courage and patience, bringing back to his dripping tent dreams of battle and of advancing marches, with flying colors floating over the Prussian trenches.

An order of the day from Marshal
Bazaine put an end to these illusions.
One morning Hornus on awakening
found the whole camp clamorous,
groups of soldiers in great excitement, uttering cries of rage, all shaking their fists towards one side of the
town as though their anger were
roused against some criminal. There
were shouts of " Away with him ! "
" Let him be shot ! "   And the officers did nothing to prevent them.
They kept apart with bent heads as
if ashamed of being seen by their men.
It was indeed shameful. The Marshal's order had just been read to
150,000 fighting men, well armed and
still efficient—an order which sur-
rendered them to the enemy without
a struggle !

" And the colors ? " asked Hornus,
growing pale.   The colors were to be

given up with the rest, with the arms,
with what was left of the munitions
of war—everything.

" *To-To-Tonnerre de Dieu!* " stut-
tered the poor man. " They shan't
have mine." And he started at a run
towards the town.

IV.

HERE also there was great dis-
turbance : National Guards, civilians,
gardes mobiles shouting and excited,
deputations on their way to the Marshal ; but of this Hornus saw and
heard nothing. All the way up the
Rue du Faubourg he kept saying to
himself :

" Take my flag from me indeed !
It is not possible. They have no
right to it ! Let him give the Prussians what is his own, his gilded

carriages, his fine plate brought from
Mexico! But that, it is mine. It is
my honor. I defy any one to touch
it."

These fragments of speech were
broken by his rapid pace and by his
stammer, but the old fellow had his
idea notwithstanding; a very clear
and defined idea—to get the standard,
carry it to the regiment, and cut his
way through the Prussians with all
who would follow him.

When he reached his destination
he was not even allowed to enter the
house. The colonel, furious himself,
would see no one; but Hornus was
not to be put off thus.

He swore, shouted, hustled the
orderly!

" My flag, I want my flag." At
last a window opened.

" Is it you, Hornus ? "

"Yes, Colonel; I——"

"The colors are all at the arsenal—you have only to go there and you will get an acknowledgment."

"An • acknowledgment! What for?"

"It is the Marshal's order."

"But Colonel——"

"Leave me alone," and the window was shut.

Old Hornus staggered like a drunken man.

"An acknowledgment, an acknowledgment," he repeated mechanically, moving slowly away, comprehending only one thing, that the flag was at the arsenal and that he must get it again, no matter at what price.

V.

THE gates of the arsenal were wide
open, to allow the passage of the
Prussian wagons which were drawn
up in the yard. Hormus shuddered.
All the other ensigns were there,
fifty or sixty officers silent and sor-
rowful; those sombre carts in the
rain, with the men grouped bare-
headed behind them, had all the
aspect of a funeral.

In a corner the colors of Bazaine's
army lay in a confused heap on the
muddy pavement. Nothing could be
sadder than these bits of gay-colored
silks, these ends of gold fringe and
of ornamented hafts, all this glorious
paraphernalia thrown on the ground,
soiled by rain and mud. An officer
took them one by one, and as each

regiment was named, its ensign advanced to receive an acknowledgment. Two Prussian officers, stiff
and unmoved, superintended the
ceremony.

And must you go thus, oh sacred
and glorious flags!—displaying your
brave rents, sweeping the ground
sadly like broken-winged birds, with
the shame of beautiful things sullied?
With each of you goes a part of
France. The sun of long marches
hid in your faded folds. In each
mark of a ball you kept the memory
of the unknown dead falling at random
around the standard, the enemy's
mark!

" Hornus, it is your turn, they are
calling you ; go for your receipt."

What did he care about a receipt!

The flag was there before him. It
was his, the most beautiful, the most

multilated of all And seeing it
again, he fancied himself once more
on that railway bank.   He heard the
whistling balls and the colonel's
voice. " *Au drapeau, mes enfants ?* "
He saw his twenty-two comrades
lying dead; himself, the twenty-third,
rushing forward in his turn to sup
port the poor flag which sank for
want of an arm. Ah! that day he
had sworn to defend it to the death—
and now!

Thinking of all this made his
héart's blood rush to his head. Dis-
tracted, mad, he sprang on the Prussian officer, tore from him his beloved
standard, tried to raise it once more
straight and high, crying " *Au-
dra*——" But the words stuck in his
throat—he felt the staff tremble, slip
through his hands. In that paralyz-
ing atmosphere that atmosphere of

death which weighs so heavily on capitulated towns, the standard could no longer float. nothing glorious could live. And old Hornus, too. choked with shame and rage, fell dead.

CHAPTER III.

ARTHUR.

OME years ago I was living near the Champs Elysées, in one of the small apartments in the back court of the Douze-Maisons. Imagine if you can such an out-of-the-way human hive in the suburbs, nestling in the midst of those big aristocratic avenues that are so cold and quiet that it seems as if one could pass them complacently only in a carriage. I do not know what whim of a proprietor, what mania of an old miser it was thus to leave in the midst of these beautiful surroundings those

empty lots and small uncultivated
gardens ; those low houses, all lop-
sided with creaky staircases on the
outside ; and their wooden verandas
full of clothes-lines, rabbit-cages, and
dozing, emaciated cats. Here lived
several households of work-people,
retired small shop-keepers, and a few
artists—the latter one finds in every
place where there are trees. There
were also here one or two boarding-
houses of sordid aspect, covered with a
crust of generations of misery. Amid
the splendor and noise of the Champs-
Elysées could be seen and heard a
continuous rolling of carriage-wheels,
a clanking of harness-chains, and the
tramp of horses' feet, filling the whole
avenue ; while the slamming of front
doors and half-smothered sounds of
pianos and violins came from a long
string of grand houses with rounded

architectural curves; their windows shaded by light silk curtains, through which one could perceive the gilded candelabra and the rare flowers in the jardinières.

This dark little street of the Douze-Maisons, lighted only by a single gas-lamp at the end, was like the stage wing of some grand theatre. compared with its beautiful surroundings. All the refuse of this luxurious quarter sought shelter here; clowns in tights, English stablemen, circus-riders, two little postilions of the Hippodrome, with their twin ponies, bill-posters, goat-carriage attendants, Punch and Judy men, sweetmeat-vendors, and, last but not least, a whole tribe of professional blind men, who came back at night bearing their chairs, accordeons, and little tin money-cups. One of these " blinds "

was married while I lived there.
That meant for us a whole night of
"music"; a medley of discordant
sounds of clarionettes, flutes, hand-
organs, and accordeons, in which one
could easily recognize every bridge
of Paris by the different melodies.
Generally, however, the passage was
as quiet as the majority of its resi-
dents, who, as I have said, came back
after night-fall and were too tired to
be noisy.

But late Saturday night there was
always sure to be a great racket in
the street, for it was then that Arthur received his week's pay.

Arthur was my neighbor.

A low wall, covered by a clinging
vine, was the only separation between
my apartment and the furnished
rooms in which he lived with his
wife and children. Therefore, in

4

spite of myself, his life was to a certain extent mixed with mine, and every Saturday night I heard without a chance of missing the least item, the horrible Parisian drama enacted in that household of work-people.

It would always begin in the same manner; the wife making ready the dinner while the children stood around, she talking to them while busy preparing the evening meal. The clock would strike seven and then eight o'clock, and still no Arthur had come. As the time passed, her voice would change in tone and become pathetic and full of tears. The children would get hungry and sleepy and begin to cry, and as the father had not yet come they would eat without him and then go to bed and sleep like a lot of little chickens.

The mother would come out on
the piazza and mutter between sobs,
" Oh, the scoundrel, the scoundrel!"
Neighbors coming home would see
her there and say, sometimes pity-
ingly :

" Why don't you go to bed, Mrs.
Arthur? You know he will not
come home, as it is his pay-night."

Sometimes, they would linger
awhile, mixing a little advice with
much gossip.

" If I were you, I would do so and
so."

" Why don't you tell his em-
ployer?"

" Your father ought not to allow
it," etc., etc., till they had exhausted
their stock of remedies for such cases
as hers.

But all this pity and advice would
only make her cry and lament the

more. She would still persist in her
hope, in her waiting, until completely ·
unnerved.

At last the street would become
quiet, and all doors would close. but
she still remained there with but the
one idea, relating to herself, and alone.
all her sorrows, with that abandon of
the lower classes which always lives
half its life in the street. She would
speak of rent behind, of creditors
tormenting her, the baker refusing
bread.

What would she do if he again
came home without his money?

At last, overcome with fatigue, exhausted by watching belated passers-
by, she would go in. Long after,
when I thought everything was quiet,
I would hear her cough. She was
again on the stoop, brought back by
anxiety, straining her eyes to look

down the black street and seeing
nothing there but misery and distress.

Towards one or two o'clock, and
often later, some one would ring at
the end of the passage. It was
Arthur coming home. Usually he
had a companion, dragging him to
the very door and urging him to
enter. Then he would loiter around,
undecided whether to enter as yet,
well knowing the reception that
awaited him.

In climbing the stairs to his rooms,
the silent house, sending back the
sounds of his heavy footsteps, like so
many remorses, seemed to embarrass
him. He would stop before every one
of those misery-hovels, on his way
up, and shout: " Good-evening,
Madame Weber ; " or " Good-night,
Madame Mathieu." Then if he re-

ceived no answer he would fling at
them an assortment of vile epithets
and oaths until every one in the
neighborhood had been aroused, and
the doors and windows, open to
answer him with insults and curses.
That was exactly what he was waiting for. The wine he had drunk
seemed to provoke quarrels and fights.
When he had once worked himself
into a rage then he had no fear in
going home.

That home-coming was the climax
of the affair. Approaching his door,
he would find it locked and then he
would shout: "Open! It is I !" Then
I would hear the bare feet of the wife
on the cold tiles ; the scratching of
matches ; and, at last, the opening
of the door. The man on entering
would begin stammering out his
story, always the same. He had

met comrade so and so, who worked
on the railroad, or at the wharf, and
they had spent the evening together.
The woman would not even listen,
but would interrupt him repeatedly
with inquiries for money. At last he
would answer :

"The money? Oh, I haven't any
left, you know I——"

"You lie!"

He was indeed lying. Even in the
excitement of his debauch he would
always reserve a few sous, thinking
of the great thirst which would tor-
ment him on the following Monday.
It was that small remainder of his
pay which his wife was now trying to
get from him.

She would hang on him, shake him,
search him, and turn all his pockets
inside out. After a few moments I
would hear the money rolling over

the tiles and the woman throwing
herself on it in triumphant glee.

Then I would hear swearing and
smothered blows.   The drunkard
was revenging himself.   Once beginning to beat her, he would not stop.
The terrible suburban wines which
he had imbibed, by this time mounted
to his brain, had now crazed him.
The woman would howl, the furniture
would be smashed, the children would
begin screaming, and then in the
street the windows and doors would
fly open again and I would hear:

" It's only Arthur."   " He's making
a bigger row though than ever," and
such-like remarks.

Sometimes the father-in-law, an old
rag-picker living in the next room,
would come to his daughter's assist-
ance.   Arthur would lock the door so
as not to be disturbed in his opera-

tions, and then a most sickening and horrible dialogue would take place through the keyhole.

"Haven't you had enough, with your two years in jail?" the old man would cry. Then the drunkard would reply in bantering tones:

"Well, yes, I have been in prison two years, but what of that? I've paid my debt to society; when will you pay yours?"

But if the old man would again speak of the prison-episode and dwell too long on that fact, Arthur would angrily open the door and fall heavily over his father-in-law, mother-in-law, and neighbors who had collected on the landing outside. Then would ensue a general *mêlée*, after which Arthur would be carefully picked up and put to bed, to sleep off his debauch.

Yet, with all this, he was not a bad man. Often on Sunday, the day following those awful scenes, the drunkard, now appeased, without a cent with which to buy drink, would spend the day at home. They would bring the chairs out of their rooms and spend the day on the balcony.

Madame Weber, Madame Mathieu, and the whole house would congregate there, and they would talk and gossip; Arthur of course being their leader.

You would have thought him one of those model working-men who patronize night-schools. He would speak in a low soft voice, eloquently putting forth fragments of ideas, which he had caught here and there, upon the rights of the working classes and the tyranny of capitalists. His poor wife, subdued by the beating of the previous night, would look at him with new admiration, forgetting the wrongs he had inflicted on her.

The neighbors would ask him to sing, and he would render in his throaty voice full of false tears, " Les Hirondelles " by Belanger. Oh ! that voice, and the stupid sentimentalism of the lower classes. It was enough to drive all but his devoted listeners indoors.

The neighbors looked tearfully out at the pale blue sky as Arthur finished, and wondered if he would now become the ideal man of their kind.

But no ; this little scene of softness did not prevent him from coming home drunk the next Saturday night to beat his wife anew and arouse the neighborhood.

There, in the midst of that misery, was a small army of other Arthurs, waiting but for the years to pass that they might be old enough to drink their pay and beat their wives too.

And it is such a race that wishes to govern the world.   " Ah, the evil of it!" as my neighbors of the passage would say.

CHAPTER IV.

DREAMS.

AS it ever happened to you to start out from home with light step and buoyant heart, and after a two-hours walk in the streets of Paris to return depressed and anxious, with a sudden and unaccountable sadness? On such an occasion you say to yourself : " What ails me? what is the matter? " but you find nothing, search as you may. Your walk has been pleasant, the sidewalks dry, the sun warm ; and yet you experience such a painful anxiety, that weighs upon

you like the impress of a newly-felt sorrow.

It is because in big Paris the crowd feels itself free and unobserved, so that one cannot walk a single step without encountering some fearful distress which, in coming in contact with, leaves its mark upon one. I do not speak solely of familiar misfortunes, the troubles of our friends, or the cares of people indifferent to us, to which we lend but a reluctant ear, but which nevertheless grieve us in spite of ourselves. I speak of afflictions, total strangers to us, of which we get but a glimpse, here and there, for one moment only perhaps, in the midst of our preoccupied walks and the bustle and confusion of the streets. They are either fragments of dialogues jerked out by passing carriages, deaf and blind preoccupations speaking to themselves and aloud, tired shoulders, wild gestures, feverish eyes, pallid faces swelled with tears, recent mournings clothed in black. And then, other slight details, scarcely noticeable ! A frayed collar, brushed, oh how often ! a velvet ribbon at the neck of a poor hunchback girl and cruelly and carelessly tied right between her deformed shoulders. All the visions of unknown misfortunes, passing quickly, which you forget almost immediately. But you have felt the swift touch of their sadness, your clothes have received the imprint of the misery they drag after themselves ; and at the end of the day, you feel that everything emotional your heart contains has been unconsciously touched, for you have been caught either at a street-corner or on some threshold by the invisible

thread which connects all misfortunes
and sets them in motion at the least
contact.

I was thinking of that the other
morning (for it is especially in the
morning that Paris shows its misery),
watching a poor devil walking in
front of me.   His ill-fitting, shrunken
trousers and thin overcoat seemed to
exaggerate his gestures ; while his
big strides keeping pace with his
big ideas, were all the more grotesque.
Bent in two, his limbs crooked like
those of an old tree during a heavy
storm, the man was walking rapidly.
Now and then his hand would dive
into one of his coat-pockets and
would take out a half-cent roll he
was munching furtively, as if ashamed
to be seen eating in the street.

Bricklayers and other working
people generally give me an appetite

when I see them, seated on the sidewalk, bite into their scant though
fresh crust. The office-boys also make
me envious, running from the bakery
to their offices, with a pen behind
their ears, their mouths full, and re-
joicing in their open-air meal.

But here one could feel the shame
of real hunger; and it was such a
pity to watch the poor creature, daring to eat his bread by stealth and
only a few crumbs at a time.

i had been following him for a
good while, when suddenly, as it
often happens in those uncertain
lives, he seemed to change his mind
with his direction, and, turning about,
found himself face to face with me.

"Ha! here you are! It is you."

By chance I knew him a little. He
was one of those, business pro-
moters of which there are so many

5

in Paris, inventors, founders of
impossible dailies, etc., about whom,
for some time past, there has been
much spoken, and written, and who,
for three months previously, had
disappeared entirely from view. A
few days after he had taken himself
off, nobody spoke of him or gave
him a thought. Seeing me, he became confused, and so as to cut short
all questions, and probably also to
avert my attention from the sordid
aspect of his clothes, as well as from
the roll he was eating, he began to
speak in a rapid and mock-joyous
strain. . . . Business was getting
along well, really splendidly now.
. . . It was only for a few days he
had been embarrassed. . . . But now,
he had got hold of a magnificent
thing. . . . A big industrial illus-
trated paper. . . . A great deal of

money in it . . . famous advertising
contracts ! . . . And his face was
full of animation as he spoke. He
seemed to have grown taller. Little
by little he assumed the air of a
patron towards me, as if already in
his editorial office, and he went even
so far as to ask me for contributions :
" And you know, it is such a sure
thing," he added, with a triumphal
air. " I am beginning with three
hundred thousand francs Girardin
promised me ! "

Girardin !

It is always that name that comes
first to those visionaries. When it
is pronounced in my hearing it is as
if I saw new cities, big unfinished
buildings, freshly printed journals
with long lists of stockholders and
directors. How often have I heard
them say, speaking of impossible

schemes : " We must speak to Girardin about this." And to him also,
the poor creature, this idea of speaking
to Girardin about it had come. All
night long, probably, he had prepared
his plans, made his estimates, then he
had gone out, and thinking it over
while eating his bread, the whole
thing had become so beautiful, that
when we met it appeared impossible
to him that Girardin could refuse " the
three hundred thousand francs."
In saying that the money had been
promised him, the unfortunate man
was not lying ; he was but continuing
his idle dream.

While talking, we were pushed
along by the crowd. It was on the
sidewalk of one of the busy streets
that run from the Exchange to the
Bank of France, full of absent-
minded people busy with their affairs ;

anxious shopkeepers hurrying to pay
their notes, small brokers with ill-
looking faces, whispering figures in
each other's ear in passing. And to
hear his beautiful plans in the midst
of this crowd, in this place of specu-
lators, where one feels the haste and
fever of chance-games, it gave me
the shivers, as if he had told me the
story of a shipwreck out on the open
sea. I could really see before me all
the man was telling me—see his ca-
tastrophes upon other faces, and his
radiant hopes in others' wild looks.
He left me as abruptly as he had
accosted me, thrown once more into
the whirl and folly of dreams, of lies,
which those people term with such
serious faces " business."

Five minutes later, I had forgotten
him. But, in the evening, when I
reached home, as I was shaking off

with its misery the street's dust, there
rose before me a pale, painfully
pinched face, with a small piece of
bread in his hand, and I still could
see his gesture when he emphasized
those pompous words: "With the
three hundred thousand francs Girardin promised me!"

CHAPTER V.

VOYAGE CIRCULAIRE.

T is eight days since Lucien Bérard and Hortense Larivière were married. Madame veuve Larivière, the mother, has for thirty years past kept a toy-shop in the Rue de la Chaussée-d'Antin.

She is a stiff, sharp woman, with an overbearing temper, and not having been able to refuse her daughter to Lucien, the only son of a hardwareman of the quarter, she intends keeping a close watch over the young couple. Although by the contract

she has relinquished the toy-shop to
Hortense, reserving to herself a room
only in the apartment, she still, in
fact, manages the house, under pre-
tence of showing the children the
details of the business.

We are in August, the heat is intense and transactions are very dull.
Madame Larivière is, of course, more
sour than ever. She will not allow
Lucien to forget himself even a moment when beside Hortense. Did
she not find them one morning kissing each other in the shop! A
proper thing to be sure, and likely to
bring customers to the place. She
had never allowed M. Larivière to
touch her so much as with the tips of
his fingers during business hours.
He, it is true, never dreamt of such a
thing. And that is how they had
built up a business.

Lucien, not daring as yet to revolt, sends kisses to his wife when his step-mother's back is turned. One day, however, he plucked up courage enough to remind her that the families, previous to the wedding, had promised them a honey-moon trip. At this Madame Larivière puckered her thin lips.

"Well," she said, "take an afternoon walk in the Bois de Vincennes."

The newly-married pair looked at each other dumfounded.

Hortense now begins to find her mother really ridiculous. Even at night she can, scarce be left alone with her husband. At the least noise, up comes Madame Larivière in her bare feet, who knocks at the door to ask if they are not ill. And when they answer that they enjoy the best of health, she exclaims :

" You had better go to sleep then.
. . . I'll catch you again napping to-
morrow behind the counter."

It is past endurance.

Lucien instances all the shop-
keepers in the quarter who take short
trips, while relations or trusty assist-
ants are left behind to mind the shop.
There is the dealer in gloves at the
corner of the Rue Lafayette who is at
Dieppe, the cutler of the Rue Saint-
Nicolas who has just left for Luchon,
the jeweler near the Boulevard who
has taken his wife to Switzerland.
Nowadays anyone who is anything
allows himself a month's holiday.

" 'Tis the end of all business, monsieur, do you hear?" exclaims Madame Larivière. " In the time of M.
Larivière, we went once a year, on
Easter Monday, to the Bois de Vincennes, and we were none the worse

off for it! Shall I tell you what it is? You will be the ruin of the house with tastes for voyaging like this! Yes, the house is ruined."

" But it was well understood we should have a trip somewhere," put in Hortense. " Remember, mamma, you said so."

" Perhaps I did, but that was before the wedding. . . . One is apt to say all sorts of nonsense before the wedding. What? Come, now, let us be serious."

Lucien walks out to avoid a quarrel. He harbors a ferocious inclination to throttle his step-mother. When he returns, however, after two hours' absence, he is quite another man, speaks in a soft voice to Madame Larivière and has a queer smile at the corner of his mouth.

In the evening, he asks his wife:

" Have you ever been in Normandy ? "

" Of course you know I haven't,"
says Hortense. " I have never been
anywhere except to the Bois de Vincennes."

The following day, a thunderbolt
burst in the toy-shop. Lucien's
father, père Bérard, as he is called in
the quarter, where he is known for a
bon-vivant with a sharp-eye to business, calls round and invites himself
to breakfast. When coffee comes on
the table, he exclaims :

" I've brought our children a present," and triumphantly produces two
railway tickets.

" What's that ? " inquires the step-
mother in a husky voice.

" Two first-class places for a circular
tour in Normandy. . . Well, my little
ones, what do you say to that ?   A

whole month of fresh air! You'll come back fresh as roses."

Madame Larivière is astounded. She has a mind to protest, but does not care to pick a quarrel with père Bérard, who has always the last word. But when she hears the hardwareman speak of taking the travellers at once to the station, her amazement exceeds all bounds. He won't loosen his grip of them till he sees both off in the train.

" Very well," she mutters with inward rage, " take my daughter away from me. So much the better; they won't be kissing each other in the shop at least, and I can look after the honor of the house."

At last the married couple reach the Saint-Lazare station, accompanied by their step-father, who has barely given them time to throw some linen and clothing into a trunk. He bestows sonorous kisses on their cheeks, advises them to see everything, and tell him all about it when they come back. 'Twill amuse him.

On the landing where the train takes its departure, Lucien and Hortense hurry along in quest of an empty carriage. They have the good luck to find one; they jump into it and are just preparing for a tête-à-tête, when to their mortification a spectacled gentleman gets into the same compartment, who, as soon as seated, looks at them severely. The train starts; Hortense with a heavy heart turns her head and affects to scan the landscape; but tears well up into her eyes so that she cannot see even the trees outside. Lucien tries to hit on some ingenious plan where-by to get rid of the old gentleman, but his expedients are too high-handed.

A moment he hopes their follow-traveller will get down at Melun or Verdun, but he soon finds out his mistake; the gentleman is bound all the way to Havre. Lucien exasperated decides to take his wife's hand in his; they are married after all, and may openly avow their fondness. But the old gentleman's brow lowers more and **more**; it is evident he disapproves altogether any such outward mark of affection; so the young woman, blushing, withdraws her hand. The rest of the journey is got throught with constraint and in silence.

Happily they are now at Rouen.

Lucien bought a guide-book on leaving Paris. They alight at an hotel which is recommended, and

become a prey to the waiters. At
the table d'hôte they scarce dare exchange a word before the crowd of
people staring at them. So they
retire early to rest; but the partition
walls are so thin, that the neighbors
to left and right cannot budge without their being made aware of it.
They no longer dare to move or even
cough in their beds.

"Let us go see the town," says
Lucien on rising the next morning,
"and start off quick for Havre."

They are on foot all day, visit the
cathedral, where they are shown the
Tour-de-Beurre, a tower built from
the proceeds of taxes imposed by the
clergy on the butter of the country;
go to the old palace of the Dukes of
Normandy, enter the ancient churches
now used as corn-lofts, see the Place
Jeanne-d'Arc, the Museum, even the

Monumental Cemetery. They seem to be accomplishing a duty, nor do they neglect to look at every historic house. Hortense is especially bored to death, and gets so tired that she falls asleep in the train the next day.

On reaching Havre, a fresh annoyance greets them. At the hotel where they get down, the beds are so narrow that they must needs take a room with double bedsteads. Hortense feels this almost as an insult, and sheds tears. Lucien consoles her as best he can, assuring her that they shall stay at Havre no longer than is just necessary to see the town. And their wild walks recommence.

Then they quit Havre, and stop for a few days at every important town set down in their itinerary. They visit Honfleur, Pont-l'Evêque,

6

Caen, Bayeux. Cherbourg ; their heads get crammed with such a rigmarole of streets and monuments and churches that they confuse the whole, and grow dizzy with the rapid succession of a set of horizons devoid of all interest to them.

They no longer look at anything, keeping the tenor of their way, strictly as it were a task they know not how to get rid of: Since they have set out, they must needs somehow find their way back. One evening, at Cherbourg. Lucien let fall this ominous expression of his views: " I think I like your mother's place better."

The next day they start for Granville. Lucien remains sombre and casts wild eyes over the country, where fields on each side the carriage expand to view like a fan. Sud-

denly, as the train comes to a stop at
a small station, the name of which
does not reach their ear, but where a
lovely corner of verdure is seen among
the trees, Lucien cries out : " Get
down, my dear, get down quick ! "

" But this is no station marked on
the guide-book." expostulates Hortense.

" The guide-book, say you ? Wait
a bit, I'll show you what we'll do
with the guide-book ! Come, quick,
get down."

" What about the luggage ? "

" A fillip for the luggage ! " .

And Hortense did get down, the
train started and left them both in
the lovely corner of verdure. On
leaving the station, they were in the
open country. Not a sound. Birds
were singing in the trees; a clear
stream flowed at the bottom of the

vale. Lucien's first care was to fling the guide-book into the middle of a pool of water as they went by. At last, it is over; they are free.

Three hundred steps off stands a secluded auberge or country-inn, where the housewife gives them a large room as cheerful to look at as sunshine in spring. The white-washed walls are a yard thick. Besides, there is not a traveller in the house, and the hens alone look at them with an inquisitive air.

"Our tickets are good for eight days yet," says Lucien. "We'll spend the eight days here."

What a delightful week! They go off in the morning by untrod paths, dive into the depths of a wood on the slope of a hill, and there spend the livelong day, lost among the tall grasses that hide their youthful love.

Anon they follow the stream; Hortense runs like an escaped schoolgirl, or pulls off her bottines and takes a footpath, while Lucien provokes her, so that she utters little screams when he comes up suddenly behind and smacks a kiss on the back of her neck. Their lack of linen, and dearth of everything generally, is highly amusing; they are, indeed, elated beyond measure to be thus left to themselves in a desert where none may think of looking for them.

Hortense has been obliged to loan some of the housewife's country underclothing, and the coarse stuff scratches her skin and makes her giggle. Their room is so gay! They lock themselves in at eight o'clock, when the dark, silent country no longer tempts them out. They give special directions not to be woke up

too early. Lucien at times goes
downstairs in his slippers and brings
up the breakfast, eggs and cutlets,
allowing no one to enter the room.
And the breakfast is exquisite thus
eaten on the bedside and endless
from the kisses which outnumber
the mouthfuls of bread. The seventh
day they are surprised and desolate
to find that they have lived through
the week so rapidly. And so they
take their departure as they came,
without even wishing to be told the
name of the country where they have
loved.

Now at least they have had a
quarter of their honeymoon. Not
until they reach Paris do they come
across their luggage. When, however, père Bérard questions them as
to their trip, they get mixed up.
They saw the sea at Caen, and locate

the Tour-de-Beurre at Havre. "The deuce!" exclaims the hardwareman; "but you don't say a word about Cherbourg. . . What of the Arsenal?"

"Oh! a wee bit of an arsenal," quietly responds Lucien : "it lacks trees."

At which Madame Larivière, still sulky, shrugs her shoulders, and mutters: "'Tis worth one's while to go voyaging! why they don't even know what monuments they've seen. . . . Come, Hortense, enough of this : go to the counter, please."

CHAPTER VI.

IN THE STUDIO.

I.

"OMEN certainly are a horrid invention!

"How I wish that a Black Plague or a second Deluge would carry you all off! What an abode of peace, what an oasis this world would then be!"

This chivalrous amiable sentiment. is uttered by my cousin, a fine young man of five-and-twenty, about six-foot-two in height, and with an eye-glass always stuck in his eye, which seems to expand when he gives vent

88

to ferocious invectives against my sex.. The above philippic is provoked by my determination to go and spend a few months in Paris in order to study painting at Madame Latour's *atelier*. I had been meditating some time upon this move, when a letter received that morning from my friend Olga Soultikoff, a young Russian, then in Paris, chiefly for painting purposes, decided me. This is the letter, which unfortunately, I had read to my cousin :

> " Chez Madame Dupont,
> " Quai des Grands Augustine, Paris.

" My dear Louisa,—You must keep the promise you made me to come and spend some time in

> ' Ce cher pays de France,
> Berceau de ton enfance.'

Come at once, to brightness and sun-

shine. How can you remain so long
in dreary, dirty, dismal, damp, de-
pressing London ? where the sun only
shines through a thick yellow flannel
dressing-gown, as if that luminary
suffered from a cold in his head and
gets up late, well muffled in blan-
kets.

" The London climate has upon me
the effect of a pall, and the dismal
grandeur, contrasted with the hideous
poverty, makes me shudder. There
is no lightness, no *abandon*, no grace ;
nobody seems to care for anybody
else, and everybody tries to outshine
his neighbor. Still there is much
goodness in old England : roast beef,
porter, and plum-pudding are the
emblems of Great Britain ; solid,
heavy, respectable, wholesome. Perhaps champagne may be typical of
France : light, airy, intoxicating ; but

my artistic temperament prefers this
to the respectable heaviness of England.

"However, I must not speak too
harshly about that mighty country,
as I have only spent a few months
there. Italy and France are the
Promised Lands of the artist nature.
This is a delightful *pension*, not
far from the Louvre—that sanctuary
consecrated to the *chefs-d'œuvre* of
the great old masters! Madame
Dupont is a nice little woman; never
interferes with anybody, never asks
indiscreet questions; *enfin*, this is
Liberty Hall. There is a live Genius
flourishing here, or rather, like most
geniuses, on the brink of ruin. He
wears his hair long, dresses very
shabbily, has holes in his wide-awake
—for the sake of ventilation, he
declares; he is stuffed with queer,

strong, artistic ideas, and he and I
are great friends.

" There are about forty boarders,
most of them odd, but come and
judge for yourself. I go to Madame
Latour's studio; she is a great artist,
coloring gorgeous, worthy of Rubens
or Correggio ; she is also a musician
and a mathematician, is *originale*
and eccentric, and is separated from
her husband, simply because Monsieur
Latour bored her and was always
prowling about her studio; so she
told him that her apartment was
too small and he had better go
off.

" The meek husband obeyed, and he
is now in Belgium, quite happy, for
he fears his artist wife. They had
one child, but Madame Latour one
day, in a fit of absence of mind, sat
upon her baby, and, as she is a very

stout woman, the baby never recovered
being sat upon, and died a few days
after. She did not feel the loss much,
and now lives but for art; her
enthusiasm, her love, are concentrated
in that. In her early youth she
loved passionately, was deceived, and
so she threw her mind, her soul, her
very body, into her painting. If I
were a man, I should be devoted to
such a woman.

"She has so much soul, so much
power; her great black eyes shine
like seas of light, with that sacred
fire which seems to consume her.
Such women are rare because genius
is rare. Madame Latour, though a
genius, is fond of the pomps and
vanities of this wicked world; she
intends giving a grand fancy ball in
six weeks from this, and I want you
particularly to be there. Write at

once to let me know what day I am
to expect you, and do not be per-
suaded into not coming by that cousin
of yours.   Is he still a woman-hater?
Au fond, I think he loves us all too
much, and that to conceal his tender
heart he puts on an armor of cynicism and indifference.

　　　" Your affectionate friend,
　　　　　　" OLGA SOULTIKOFF.

" P.S.—Tell your cousin that I
heard that he is already much in
love.   I am glad to hear it, for when
he is married he will think better of
all women, and will espouse our
cause, stand up for and discuss our
right and our wrongs, perhaps vote
for our having the franchise."

My cousin Horace scowls atro-
ciously over this *post scriptum*.

"Fall in love indeed! No one will ever find me suffering from that complaint."

"But you are certain to be in that condition some day or other, and the attack will be bad; for love is like the measles; if you get it early in life you recover easily, but once on the shady side of thirty you will suffer terribly."

"There might have been some danger for me if I had lived a century ago, when there were a few charming woman on the earth—quiet, innocent beings, satisfied with the sphere of home duties; but now they are merely amphibious creatures struggling to the front, wanting to take our place, to govern the world, to vote, to become doctors, clergymen—I hate them all!

"There is an open antagonism be-

tween the sexes, an uncivil war. And
you, instead of keeping in your orbit,
which means happiness, want to join
that horrid faction of strong-minded
females—a third sex, a social excres-
cence. Do not be a blooming idiot.
Remain at home ; you are more likely
to marry than if you scamper about the
Continent and become an artist. Men
do not like independent women ; we
do not want to be ruled by our wives.
Women ought to have the qualities
which are generally wanting in men ;
to complete us, as it were."

"Ah ! you are getting afraid of us.
You lords of the creation, you do not
like to look up to, but down upon us ;
but surely, Horace, you could not
respect me if I remained at home forever, tatting and tatting, with a kind
of label all over me, ' Waiting to be
married. Fragile.' I know a woman

who hates her sex ; her advice is,
matrimony, *coûte que coûte.*"

" Burn them alive," growls Horace,
his eyeglass getting to look wicked
and large, " and I think that I should
begin with Mademoiselle Olga.

" She is a dangerous young person,
very *exaltée*, enthusiastic, wild—an
undetected young lunatic ; but I am
sorry, though, for her ; she is young,
alone, and extremely pretty," adds my
cousin, relenting, and the eyeglass
slips off.   " She is an orphan too, poor
girl ! no one to look after her. But
you have no excuse, so I advise you
to remain and take plenty of exercise,
for you seem to me to be expanding
fearfully, and that may spoil your
chances in life."

Now this is a stab, a Parthian shot.
The skeleton in my closet is the dread
of growing like Falstaff, or a niore.

7

recent hero. I had tried Banting,
but to no effect. However, I do not
betray my mortification, only shrug
my shoulders, leave the room in order
not to hear any more unpleasant truths,
and write off to Olga ; for if a thing
has to be done let it be done quickly.
Then I go out and post the letter, for
I never believe that my letters reach
their destination unless I drop them
with my own hands into the letter-
box.

*   *   *   *

It is with a mixed sensation of
pleasure and regret that later on I
find myself at the station alone !

A sense of loneliness creeps over me.
I almost wish to be back in the snug
drawing-room, listening to Horace's
invectives and sermons. Here all
is turmoil, life, bustle, glare, glitter,
restlessness, noise of cabs, porters

rushing about with big trunks, everybody and everything hurrying to and
fro. Suddenly I hear my name
called out, two arms are round my
neck, and there stands bright, pretty
little Olga, accompanied by two
gentlemen.

" So delighted to see you, *chérie!*
Welcome to la belle France ! Let
me introduce you to two of my friends
who are staying at the boarding-house
—both Englishmen—Mr. Morris and
Mr. Blake."

We all shake hands.

" Mr. Morris is evidently the
Genius." I mentally ejaculate ; he
looks helpless, bewildered, and inspired ; he wears a velveteen coat
quite clean, and his wideawake is
guiltless of holes ; he is rather handsome, very dark, just a dash of the
demon about him.

Mr. Blake is a contrast—a short, spruce, dapper little figure, dressed most carefully, quite *un petit maître ;* he has a lovely white flower in his buttonhole, and looks as if he had just stepped out of a bandbox.

I confide my keys to him, and he politely goes off and looks after my luggage, which has to undergo the process of being examined.

" Now, Mr. Morris, won't you go and get us a *voiture ?* " says Olga, in her sweet, foreign accent. " I do wonder if he will be able to do that ; for of course you have guessed that he is the Genius, always up in the heights—a great deal of power about him, but not much practicality."

But Olga's remarks are cut short by the reappearance of Mr. Blake, followed by a porter carrying my trunk.

" The *fiacre* is waiting. What a wonder that it is not a hearse ! " exclaims Mr. Blake, with a shrug of compassion. " I did not think that Morris could discern one vehicle from another."

The trunk is placed on the roof, my innumerable parcels fill up nearly the cab, Olga and I squeeze into a corner, and the two men bid us good-evening.

Off we rattle through the brilliant streets. It is a lovely evening in May, the trees are clothed in delicate young green, the stars are just beginning to shine, the shops are beautifully lit, the streets are crowded. How poetical Paris looks from the Place de la Concorde on to the bridge !

The towers of Notre Dame and of St. Jacques la Boucherie, standing there like guardian angels protecting the

beloved city. The dismal prison of
the Conciergerie, the ruins of the Tuileries, lend a solemnity to the scene.
The Seine is twinkling with many
lights, the bathing-houses are slightly
lit up, giving it a weird appearance.
A few dark barges are gliding warily
by, like dreary, troubled spirits. The
equestrian statue of Henri Quatre
looks well in the evening light—the
gay monarch there in effigy watching
over his dear Paris. At last the cab
stops.

Olga rings a bell ; the door is opened
by a neat *bonne* in a very white cap
and apron, holding a brass candlestick.
The *bonne* ushers us into a large sitting-room furnished with crimson
curtains, chairs, etc., gilt clock and
ornaments on the mantelpiece; and
the floor is so highly waxed that it
is almost impossible to walk without

slipping. A tiny lady in black silk comes forward.

" This is my friend, Miss Louisa Larcom," says Olga in French.

Madame Dupont makes a graceful *révérence*, is enchanted to see me, inquires after my journey, and says that she will send me up *du thé* in my room.

Olga says that I shall have tea with her in her own sitting-room. So, bidding the little lady good-night, we go upstairs to Olga's apartment.

" What a lovely *sanctum sanctorum!*" I exclaim ; and certainly it is a charming room worth describing. The furniture is of bright blue damask silk, white lace curtains, and the *fond* of the carpet is white, with wreaths of roses entwined with blue ribbon. A bookcase of carved oak filled with beautifully-bound books.

On all sides are statuettes of Dresden china. A Venus de Milo and a Venus de' Medici in bronze, mount guard on each side of the bookcase. A fine Erard piano stands in the middle of the room. On a rosewood easel is a study of a head in black and white just begun. Out of this is a small bedroom with a pretty bed and toilette all white. Engravings of Ary Scheffer's famous pictures—of "Les deux Mignons," "Ste.-Monique," and "St.-Augustin," decorate the walls, besides photographs of nearly all the great masterpieces in art.

"This is your room, leading out of mine." says Olga opening a door. "Of course yours is not so beautiful as mine, for mine is furnished out of my own pocket, and yours is Madame Dupont's taste. Still it is pretty and cosy, furnished in pink *perse*. You

have everything *couleur de rose*, and
I am all in the blues. Still I am not
going to exchange. Now take off
your things, and let us make ourselves comfortable. I love luxury,
ease, comfort."

So saying, she takes off her walking-
dress and puts on a delicious gray soft
cashmere dressing-gown, puts her tiny
feet into lovely velvet slippers, and
throws herself into a large arm-chair,
forces me down into another, and
rings the bell for tea.

How pretty she looks now, as she in-
dolently reclines back. She is small;
her figure is round, supple, graceful;
her skin is clear and white ; her hair,
golden and wavy, is plaited round her
small well-shaped head; her eyes are
very dark and soft, but there is often
a twinkle of mischief in them ; her
mouth is lovely and surrounded by
dimples.

"What a luxurious creature! what an epicure you are, Olga!" I exclaim, half enviously, thinking of all the gifts and good things she had. "How thoroughly happy you ought to be! You have everything you want— beauty, wealth, talent, liberty, youth. You have indeed too much of the good things of this world, you spoilt child of fortune!"

"Yes, I ought to be very happy," she slowly answers, with rather a sad smile; "and it may seem strange and ungrateful on my part to say that I am not so. Happiness is within ourselves, and not derived entirely from outward circumstances. At times I feel quite happy; at others I am low and depressed. I am lonely, for I have no one belonging to me alive. When I feel very low I rush off to Madame Latour, and her influence, the feeling of her genius, seems to put new life into me; but there is a *void* within me. I do not care for people generally, so that I now live but for myself."

A knock at the door: the *bonne* comes in with a tray full of good things, which she deposits on a table close by, inquires if we require her services, and then retires.

" But, Olga, you are sure to be loved by some one worthy of you; you are so young—only two-and-twenty."

" Yes, that is my age; still, at times I feel middle-aged, for I have had great experience of life. Of course I have inspired love, and have tasted the bitterness of it, with little of its sweets ! "

" You amaze me ! " I exclaim. " You, so admired, so *recherchée*, to talk like this !—you, who seem such

a sunbeam, such a butterfly, is it
possible that you have cause for
talking so? The bitterness of love!
—you almost make me laugh. It
seems so incongruous for such *un enfant gâté* to talk thus."

"Well, then, I shall give you a
few details about my past life; and
then you will see if all is gold that
glitters, and if I have not reason at
times to be a little *triste.* But before
I tell you my unfortunate love affair,
' let us eat, drink, and be merry.'
This is Russian tea—a treat for you."

How charming she looks, as she
gracefully pours out the delicious be-
verage from a small silver teapot into
our two cups! I cannot imagine how
so fascinating a girl can ever have had
a love disappointment. Her movements, as she rushes about the room,
remind me of those of a pet kitten--

soft, purring, graceful; the small
head is well placed on the sloping
shoulders, the eyes are so luminous,
the light hair looks like an *auréole*
of glory, shedding light around it.
Olga has a wonderful inner smile—a
smile that Leonardo da Vinci alone
could have rendered, and which he
has so inimitably painted in that
famous portrait, " La Joconde, " or
" Mona Lisa."

" We shall get on together,"
suddenly exclaims Olga, while she is
cutting me a large slice of plum cake.
" I require a certain kind of sympathy,
not pity. As a rule I hate sympathy,
for though surrounded by society I
live in my own thoughts. I have such
a horror of being bored. Liberty is
my cry—liberty of ideas, of life; no
shackles of any sort. I am a Republican at heart, and the convention-

alities of society and the lies of the world sicken me."

As she utters these words her eyes flash, her cheeks flush, and she looks like a young goddess of revolt.

Suddenly she rushes to the piano, and sings a wild Russian air, and evidently forgetting me, the tea, and everything else, pours her soul into her music. And then, in a low, tragic voice, with an intensity that appals me, she intones the " Marseillaise." It is almost terrible to hear her, her eyes seem to see beyond, and, as she utters these words,

" Amour sacré de la patrie ! "

there are tears in her very voice ; then, not to give further vent to her emotion, she rattles off " Le Sabre de mon père," Schneider's famous song, from Offenbach's " Grande Duchesse." I look at Olga with astonishment.

" You are an enigma, a sphinx, an imp, a creature from another world, are you not ? "

" Indeed I am not. I belong very much to this earth; only at times I feel so lonely, so dissatisfied with myself. with everybody and everything, that I should like to get away from myself and my thoughts, to rush off to some wild spot. be blown about by the winds of heaven. and have new thoughts and ideas driven into me. Why is there not a Lethe—a wonderful stream where one could take a plunge and forget what one wishes to forget?

" Music is an intense resource to me, for I can pour out my wrongs and give way to my many moods in music. Sometimes. when painting, I take my brush and create a grotesque demon torturing some wretched soul, and, you may laugh, but it does relieve me; or I tease my cat. I often wish that I could hire a slave, that I might bully him when those dreadful fits of revolt come over me. Of course you must be horrified, and no wonder: but how can I help it, if I have a *diavolina* within me ?—perhaps seven devils, and they all kicking inside me. I feel the wretches are there, and some days they are so powerful, that if I did not take a ride on horseback, or some very violent exercise, I should do something wicked."

"What an undisciplined young rebel you are, Olga ! "

"It is inherited," she answers. "My mother was an Italian prima donna, with a voice like Malibran. I have been told she had an unhappy home life ; her step-mother tortured her by her despotism ; her artist nature

could not stand the petty worries of
a small narrow-minded household;
she ran away, went on the stage, loved,
was deceived. Disappointed, she
married my father, who was a Russian
merchant, for his wealth. He was
(you know he died when I was quite
a child) tyrannical, but generous; so
my parents were not happy in their
short married life.

" I am the offspring of these two
widely different natures: the warm,
genial, artistic, imaginative, rebellious
Italian on one side: the cruelty,
perhaps, from my father's side. So I
am an odd mixture, and am not entirely accountable for my moods. I
would gladly be different—glad to
have no aspiration, no dreams of
happiness, no longing for ideal love,
no wish for something beyond—to be
quiet, unemotional, unimaginative,

8

and satisfied with that state of life to which I have been called. But I am talking of nothing but my horrid self. The fact is, it does me good to give vent to my inner feelings: it is a great sign of friendship, my boring you thus."

" You are not boring me; on the contrary, dear Olga, I am deeply interested, and sympathize with your nature and understand it. You are capable of feeling great unhappiness and great happiness; but you must try and discipline yourself, and not let yourself be run away with. Put a bridle on your wild feelings."

" Yes, you are very wise, Miss Minerva; and I am an ungrateful wretch. Some days, when the sun is bright, I feel so happy that I should like to live on forever and do some good; but to-day I am *agacée*, mischievous. I should like to scratch some one."

"I shall run away," I exclaim laughing. "But now be sensible, Olga, and tell me all about these little love-affairs that seem in a measure to have altered your nature; for when I knew you five years ago you had no bitterness, no cynicism."

"Well, perhaps I had better confide this tale of woe, though, as a rule, I hate talking about myself."

So, leaving the piano, she threw herself upon the soft rug, and placing her pretty perfumed head on my lap, related what follows:

"Don't you remember, four years ago, meeting at mamma's apartments on the Boulevard des Italiens a young Pole, Stanislas Marilski?"

"Oh yes, very well, for I was much struck with his appearance; he was

distingué looking, handsome, and
artistic ; but I only saw him that one
evening.   Is he the hero ?"

" Yes ; he was the first man who
inspired a new feeling.   Before I
met him I was a joyous, light, merry,
thoughtless girl, *insouciante.*   Sufficient for the day is the evil or the
good thereof, was certainly my motto.
But Stanislas Marilski's advent
changed the course of my thoughts,
and I was no longer as joyous as a
bird.   I felt that life was a mystery ;
nature was different, and art was different, from what they had been to
me before.   I felt a capacity for
greater happiness and for greater pain.
He was certainly good-looking ; but
it was not his handsome features
that attracted me, so much as the
peculiarity of his disposition and the
originality of his mind.   He was an

orphan, a rebel, a revolutionist : he believed in nothing that was past ; history was a lie to him, he cared but for the future.

"Melancholy, cynical, passionate, we were both strongly attracted towards each other the minute we met. I met him for the first time at a *bal* at the Hôtel de Ville. I had been dancing merrily about with a very insipid polite Frenchman. I was resting, enjoying thoroughly the bright scene, the music, the lights, the wonderful dresses, the diamonds ; when, looking around, I was suddenly attracted by that very pale face and those large, dark, melancholy eyes, gazing at me so keenly.

"I looked at him, and from that moment I really did feel a different being ; a new interest had come into my life. He got introduced to my

mother, called at our house; we had
long talks together—curious to say,
chiefly on political topics. But that
ceased. We used to meet out of
doors, and have long walks together
in unfrequented parts of Paris. He
told me that he loved me, but that
for a few months he could not make
a regular offer of marriage. I did
not mind that; to be cared for
by such a man was sufficient happiness. And as my mother, who was
then in extremely delicate health,
allowed me entire liberty, I saw
Stanislas every day for five months.
One day, calling at a friend's house,
she informed me that several people
had seen me walking with Mr. Marilski—that remarks were passed; so
that my friend had made inquiries;
and did I know that Mr. Marilski
was engaged to be married to a

Polish young lady?—and she mentioned the name.

"I shall never forget what I felt when she told me this horrible piece of news. The room seemed to whirl round and round; the blood rushed to my throat and head. I tried to conceal my emotion. My friend was shocked at having told me this so abruptly. To cut a long, sad story short, I wrote to Stanislas, telling him what I had just heard. I received a miserable letter from him, confessing that there was an engagement, but that he had ceased to care for the girl, and only loved me, begging me to run away with him, and that he would gladly give up everything for my sake.

"I was considering what I had better do, when I received a letter from the mother of the girl, saying that if I married Mr. Marilski it would certainly cause her daughter's death, she was so desperately attached to him; and that Stanislas' late behavior had made her seriously ill. This piece of news decided me. I broke off entirely from him, and my poor mother took me to Dresden for change of air, scene and people.

"Strange to say, that instead of dreading love, I longed for it.

"Life seemed to me so stale, dull, and unprofitable, so uninteresting without it. I did everything to forget Stanislas, to drive away his image. I did my best even to think ill of him, to picture him in a ludicrous light. I really felt as if my soul had left me, for my body simply vegetated; but I resolved to fight against my misfortune, and not allow this dull oppression to warp my existence.

Always fond of art, I resolved to devote myself to painting. I went to the Dresden Gallery, that ideal of a picture gallery, a perfect little temple; where every picture is a gem. It was at the Dresden Gallery that I met my fate number two, in the shape of an artist who was copying the same picture (curious coincidence) that I had begun—'Kinder' von C. L. Vogel.

" My easel was close to his, and from the very first he became most attentive, prepared my pallet, gave me valuable hints about the mixing of colors, how effects were produced— impossible to be kinder. He was a great contrast to Stanislas, but there was something about him which attracted me. I shall repeat to you some of his remarks, and you will judge what sort of man number two was.

" After having looked at several of
the *chefs-d'œuvre* in the Gallery, I
remarked rather petulantly to him
that he was too fond of analyzing
the different manners in which the
pictures were painted; that he was
completely absorbed by the technical
process and missed the spiritual
idea, the soul, the genius of the con-
ception. A picture to him was a kind
of plum-pudding. Why not chiefly
admire the thought, and not merely
how an effect is produced ? "

" ' You are an *exaltée* enthusiastic
young girl," he said to me after a
few hours' talk. You must calm
yourself. You have a dash of genius,
but you require a rudder. I shall be
your rudder.'

" Cool, *n'est-ce pas ?* " said Olga,
looking up at me with an arch smile.
He went on :

" 'Those high-flown ideas are very youthful. You must not allow your imagination to run away with you.' And, fixing his cold gray eyes upon me: 'I can read your character in your face, for you are very transparent. I can read the inner workings of your mind. You have suffered, young lady; you are disappointed; you are not now in your normal condition. You have been taken out of your small orbit, and you are in a feverish state, and are trying to fling yourself into another sphere. I know the sensation well, for I have been in that condition. I have loved and lost.'

" His impudence took me by storm. 'What right have you to form such a conclusion?' I said to him.

" 'Do not be offended with me; I understand your nature, and see it all in your face; do not contradict me, but take my fatherly advice, for I am over forty and know life. Fly from love; never let a man know how much you care for him. Devote yourself to Art; that will never deceive or disenchant you, and the labor you bestow upon it will be recompensed in this world. You will have hours of real joy over your own creations—that is my experience. I looked for love, and while under the fatal spell I felt intoxicated, and like the sunflower basked in sunshine; but I have never met with a being that satisfied my heart and my soul; whilst the beauties of Nature and of Art are unfailing sources of happiness.'

"Do you mean to say, Olga, that this man spoke to you thus, on so short an acquaintance?"

" Yes, exactly," she replied, slightly coloring, and tossing back her wavy hair.

" What is his name, and who is he ? "

" His name is Crawford, and he is half Irish, half English ; a very clever artist, musician and poet, with just a dash of mystery to make him interesting. We met every day for several months at the Dresden Gallery. I felt myself alive again. Mr. Crawford made it a point to copy the same picture I copied, and the hours spent in his society were hours of happiness. At times he would recite to me ballads of his own composition, weird, strange, grotesque, and full of fancy. His voice was deep, strong and yet soft. This man puzzled and fascinated me.

" Outwardly he seemed calm, con-

ceited, vain, obstinate ; at other times
he was full of tenderness, flavored
with cynicism. He had a dramatic,
powerful way of expressing himself,
and an utter absence of ideality. We
grew confidential, and I told him about
Stanislas. I do not know if he was
actuated by a feeling of jealousy or
if he really wished to cure me entirely,
but he turned the whole affair into
ridicule. 'Fancy Mr. Marilski with
a bad cold in his head, red nose, eyes
swimming, no pocket-handkerchief,
sneezing, etc. ; or, in a dozen years,
with a big stomach like an alderman,
gouty, with a dozen children! No ;
analyze the feeling, and you will find
that love is built on a very slight
foundation. You excite an interest ;
there is some objection in the way,
your imagination is at work, and that
object becomes a dire necessity as long

as you cannot possess him or her ; but
when you do possess, illusion vanishes,
love often flies, and you find yourself
tied down for life to a log.'   Though
Mr. Crawford talked to me thus, he
did everything to excite my interest
in himself : he spoke to me of his
plans, his aspirations, his doubts,
fears,—and ended by confessing that
he loved me.

"Now comes wound number two.

" One evening at an artistic party
where I went with a lady friend,
somebody mentioned Mr. Crawford's
name, speaking in great praise of his
artistic merit and general fascination.
Then somebody else remarked, and I
still hear the words as if they were
words of fire—

" ' Yes, poor fellow, what a miserable
thing for him, that wife of his being
such a confirmed drunkard! and

though separated, he cannot marry
again. There ought to be a divorce
in such cases. Married and not married ! What a sad position for a man
still in the bloom of his life.'

" 'I never knew that Crawford was
a married man,' said a fat, elderly
gentleman. 'He has dined several
times at my house in London, and I
have often asked him why he did not
enter the blessed state of matrimony ;
and he simply said he could not, and
I thought perhaps it was because his
means did not allow him.'

" 'He is very well off,' answered
speaker number one. 'I met him
yesterday, and he told me that he felt
restless and unhappy. He is getting
on splendidly as an artist. but I hear
that he has fallen in love with a pretty
girl who is studying Art and copying
at the Gallery here.'

" I could stand it no longer. Rushing off to my *chaperone*, I complained of a sick headache ; once home, I burst into tears, felt the world again to be a wide desert, and did not return to the Gallery. My mother soon after this died ; so that month was indeed a black epoch in my life, and made lovely Dresden a perfect nightmare.

" A few days after my mother's funeral, when I was trying to pack up my things in order to get away from the now hateful place, and come to Paris, where I had, at all events, a few friends, I received a long, touching letter from Mr. Crawford, telling me all about his unfortunate marriage, his love and sympathy for me.

" I wrote back to bid him adieu, and telling him that my wish was that we should never meet or correspond any more. This is the end

9

of my love stories, so you see that I
have not been lucky in that depart-
ment."

" Poor little Olga ! " I said, taking
her soft white hand in mine, " you
have indeed suffered ; but you are
still very young, and will be more
fortunate another time."

" Oh, no, no more love-affairs !
C'est fini. I have made a firm resolve
to work hard to become a great artist
if possible. Adieu to romance, it is
a waste of time—

" ' I slept and dreamt that life was beauty :
　I woke, and found that life was duty.' "

We part for the night, both of us
vowing and declaring that we should
throw ourselves heart and soul into
the Art career, and give up all idea
of marriage. " Yes," says Olga, " all
men are deceivers ; false, vain, con-

ceited, jealous, wicked, etc., etc., etc.
I shall be a nice, clever, artistic old
maid. That is my final decision."

II.

NEXT morning Olga comes into
my room, looking so sweet and fresh
in the pretty lavender muslin, and
passing her arm through mine we go
down the staircase together.

On our way to the dining-room we
meet several boarders, issuing from
their respective bedrooms. No need
to inquire after the nationality of
these beings. Alas! Englishwomen
cannot be mistaken on the Continent;
their want of taste and tact in dress
is an unmistakable badge. This
thought shot across my brain as I perceive a large family preceding us
downstairs; the mother, tremendously

stout and beefy-looking, is in ill-fitting
many-colored garments ; with such
feet ! encased in immense boots.   She
wears two large brooches, evidently
family portraits—one pinning a collar,
the other doing nothing, just for show.
Four pretty daughters follow her
closely, guiltless of any attempt at
style.   Perhaps this want of taste in
dress is made more conspicuous by
the presence of two young American
girls, elegantly attired in the very last
new fashion.

"How are you, Mademoiselle Soultikoff ?" they both exclaim, in strong
nasal accent.   "I guess this is the
friend you have been expecting all
along ?" and on receiving from Olga
an affirmative nod they shake hands
cordially with me.   "So glad to see
you.   Are you come to Paris alone?
I reckon that you are one of our sort :

you find your family an inconvenience?

" I told my people," said the elder of the two, "all very well to stay under the maternal and paternal wing when one is a chicken, but once that period over we want our liberty. How well you have fixed your hair, Mademoiselle Soultikoff. That's the style, I guess, that Mr. Morris likes. Now do not blush, no harm having a genius for an admirer, though he ought to fix himself better, cut his hair short ; but he is a lovely fellow, and you need not be ashamed of your conquest; he never takes any notice of any one but of you. You are both kindred spirits."

I could not help laughing, but Olga seemed rather annoyed and confused.

At the bottom of the staircase we

were greeted by a very fat *bonne* in a very white frilled cap; her round face beams with good nature. She stands at the door of the *salle à manger*, and as I am the last new arrival she indicates my place, which is quite at the end of the long table. Olga is near the top, and sits close to the genius, Mr. Morris.

About fifty people sit on each side of a very long table. At a sideboard the fat *bonne*, whose name is Uranie, pours out tea and coffee, with wonderful celerity, serves everybody right and left; she darts from one to another with a quickness of step that is delightful to witness; while serving she has a funny, witty repartee always ready. At my right sits an Irish girl, as I instantly discover by her rich musical brogue. She is pretty; large gray eyes and auburn

hair. Her mother sits next to her:
they are on their way home from
Italy. Opposite to me is a large tribe
of Americans. " Well ! do they call
that breakfast on this side of the
pond?" exclaims the man of the
party, putting up his eyeglass. " I
really see nothing. In our country,
madam," addressing the Irish girl, " we
have for breakfast stewed beefsteaks,
chops, tongue, ham, eggs, potatoes
dressed in a dozen different ways, oat-
meal cakes, pumpkin pie, jams, jellies,
creams, and hot bread of different
kinds; but here I just spy a few un-
happy-looking sardines and some eggs.
Call this breakfast? Well, I suppose
we must make the best of it, but I
pronounce this starvation.

" In the States we breakfast at seven
o'clock, for every man goes to business at eight; but Europe is a slow

place, and the French have nothing to do but smoke and go to *cafés*, I guess. In England we always get the same food; no variety, and everything so greasy."

The two American young ladies are flirting desperately with a fair young Englishman.

" I guess," says the prettier of the two, " that you like better travelling without your mother."

This speech is accompanied by a look that cannot be described. The young man blushes, and says that his mother is old, and naturally prefers the quiet of her country home in England.

A little higher up the table sits the funny man of the boarding-house. His name is Mr. Smiles. He is a fine, tall, good-looking man, with splendid teeth, loud voice, and such a

ringing laugh! It shakes the room,
and is so infectious that everybody
joins in it. He is sitting by the side
of a very ugly old lady with a brown
wig on one side, and we hear him all
over the room saying,

" Now, dear Mrs. Kingsley, you have
not done your hair properly this
morning; you know that it hurts my
feelings to think that you no longer
care to appear charming in my eyes.
Are you beginning to care less for
Theophilus Smiles?" And he puts
his hand on his heart, and turns his
eyes up in a sentimental comical way,
which is diverting.

Mrs. Kingsley titters and seems
pleased.

Not far from Olga sits a pretty
English girl, with brown eyes and
brown hair. This young lady is
having a hot altercation with a gentle-

man opposite, who is evidently more
amused than excited. This young
lady is a red-hot republican. She is
declaring that the only thing worth
living for is the republic; that is her
chief thought, her first principle. She
would give up life readily for that
glorious cause. She has come over to
Paris on purpose to see Gambetta.
She takes in all the American and
Spanish papers, so that she may be
well *au fait* with passing events in
republican countries. She argues
that England is republican at heart;
that the Queen is merely an orna-
ment, but that the masses are demo-
crats. Of course this speech is a
bomb-shell. Miss Hutchinson is
called to order.

The Americans scream out nasally
that royalty is mere fancy-work, and
everything and everybody appertain-

ing to it a mistake, a nuisance. Yes,
democracy is making rapid strides.
In less than twenty years the republic will be established everywhere.

Miss Hutchinson is so pleased at
finding herself thus supported that
she gets up from her chair, rushes to
the American camp, and they all
shake hands. Then Mr. Smiles sol-
emnly rises, stretches out his long
fingers, and says " Bless you, my
children."

This causes general laughter, and
for the present the discussion is at
an end.

Mr. Blake is sitting next to a nice
ladylike widow, who my pretty neighbor tells me is on the look out for a
third husband.

Breakfast is over; the boarders
disappear. I join Olga, who is still
talking to Mr. Morris. This man is

evidently under her spell : his look,
his manner, denote that profound admiration which cannot be acted. Mr.
Morris advances towards me, and
asks me if I will honor his small
studio with a visit, and accompany
Mdlle. Soultikoff. I gladly consent,
and we both follow him upstairs to
the top of this very big house.

" It is an honor that he is paying
you," whispers Olga. " He has
never, with the exception of myself,
invited any one to his studio, and
nearly all the people entreat him to
let them have a peep ; but no use.
So he is not a favorite in this house ;
people generally think him conceited.
But really he is not so : he is con-
scious of his power, and is sensitive
and refined."

Mounting a queer little back staircase we enter a kind of garret in the

roof of the house. What a delightful view ! The Seine is twinkling at
our feet ; steamers are rushing by ;
we can just see the towers of Notre
Dame and the Sainte Chapelle, the
quays, and old book stalls, and curiosity shops. The room is hung all
round with sketches in oils and water
colors.

One of the first things that attracts
my attention is the picture of a girl
in white standing in an autumnal
landscape ; the tints of the foliage
are of a golden brown, at her feet are
crisp brown leaves, while she holds
some dead leaves in her white hands.
There is a listless, lonely look in the
face, but the likeness to Olga is striking : the same graceful figure, the
same light, untidy, wavy masses of
fair hair, the same concentrated
thought, and just a tinge of sadness

in the large dark gray eyes. Same
sweetness in the mouth, but a little
more determination in the chin, and
slightly knitted eyebrows. The
painting of the face is beautiful;
there is a tenderness of treatment
which is remarkable, and the coloring
is full of harmony. The background
is a sunset, the clouds are purple and
gold.

"This picture is the only produc-
tion of mine which gives me any sort
of pleasure," says Mr. Morris; "and
I shall never part with it." And he
gives Olga a tender look, but she
does not respond to it, and calls my
attention to some of the sketches
which are sufficient to show that Mr.
Morris is a man of genius. Some
striking landscapes are lying about—
a dark pool of water, illuminated by
one streak of strong, rippling light,

long tall willows, and a stork sleeping and standing on one leg; a sea-piece, gray sky, gloomy shore, a white bird fluttering sadly over the white-crested waves; studies of rocks by moonlight, in deep purple shadows and strong silvery lights.

The charm in these various productions is the intense feeling, the pathetic striving after a something beyond —unattainable. They are the productions of a man that has evidently suffered acutely. He has, I suspect, loved deeply and has been disappointed. These are my thoughts as I see on all sides heads full of sadness, wistfulness, and even despair.

"I suppose you do not care to make money by your art?"

"No. In my opinion art is a religion, a creed, a faith. The creation of the beautiful ought to be the

highest ambition of an artist. Our
notions of the beautiful vary accord-
ing to our temperament and edu-
cation. Perfection of form, harmony
of color, depth of expression, is what
I strive to render. When I shall be
satisfied, then perhaps I shall send to
the different exhibitions."

"And now, before we leave this
delightful studio, play something on
the piano for my friend," says Olga,
opening the instrument.

"You know that I must obey my
queen," he answers, bowing; "but
as a rule I do not play for any one.
The music I enjoy is not popular, for
it is generally found incomprehen-
sible by the masses, but I firmly
believe that it will be the music of
the future. Gounod is my favorite
master."

He sits down, and after a few

strange, wild preludes, plays portions
of that ideal masterpiece, " Faust."
I feel transported into a world of
strange fancies, inhabited by mystical
visionary beings. It is all vague,
striking, original.

I am roused by Olga, who taps me
on the shoulder and tells me it is
time to leave. Mr. Morris makes us
promise to return soon again, and we
bid him *au revoir*.

" It is curious how much genius,
power, and passion are contained in
this small room, and how much *ennui*,
stupidity, nonsense, shallowness, and
gossip, inhabit the remainder of this
large house," remarks Olga, as we
descend the staircase and enter our
room. " Lunch with me in my sitting room ; I find it such a tremendous bore to assist at the general
luncheon ; one gets so tired of seeing

10

always the same people, hearing the same jokes, and eating the same food."

" Well, Yankee is right," I remark, " when he said that money is power, and gives liberty; if you had not plenty of filthy lucre you could not afford to have your own way, and eat *pâté de foie gras* in your own room instead of joining at the common table and partaking of more homely fare. I like money, though I admire Mr. Morris's views—he is so full of imagination, that he must be quite happy."

" No," answers Olga, " Mr. Morris is not really a happy man. Of course he must have moments of intense gratification, but his ideal of beauty is so elevated that he is miserable when he cannot attain it."

" There is no doubt, Olga, that

Mr. Morris is in love with you: his manner, his look show that you occupy his thoughts, and that beautiful picture is an expression of his feelings."

" Yes, I think Mr. Morris admires me very much. Why should he not do so?

" I am pretty, artistic, and with all my faults, I am attractive; but his nature is rather like mine, so I simply feel sympathy and admire his lofty views; but I have not a bit of love for him; my heart does not beat any quicker, my pulse is just the same when he approaches me. I think quite calmly of him, and would not be at all jealous if he fell in love with any other girl. He is very odd: his mother was a German, and I fancy that she was rather queer—in fact, I imagine that she was slightly insane;

he has inherited from her unhealthy,
odd notions. He has often told me
that he would rather not marry a
woman he was in love with : love is
such a strange feeling that he would
like to feel eternally the pleasure and
pain it occasions, and to enjoy the
torture of not possessing what he
longs for. It is a curious idea, but I
daresay he is right ; marriage must,
in a way, destroy the poetry of love.

"A sincere attachment and quiet
happiness follows, but many illusions
vanish. He told me, that as a young
fellow, he fell in love with a beautiful girl, who sang and danced like an
angel, and whose face was a vision of
beauty—well, she loved him ; they
met often at a country house and she
promised to marry him. Strange, the
idea frightened and disenchanted him
so much that, for fear his love should

vanish, he went away engaged to her.
In his absence, she caught a fearful
cold, and three weeks after his departure she was lying in her grave. He
was travelling about, and did not know
of her death till he returned. His
grief was intense, and still he confesses
that to him there is a melancholy
pleasure in the idea that she died
loving him entirely, without having
belonged to him. He is an eccentric
creature, and as he has frankly spoken
to me about his odd notions, he cannot expect me to wish to marry him.
He is a poet, an artist, and a musician, utterly unfitted for the prose of
married life."

III.

WHAT a clamor, clatter, and babel
of tongues!

The musical English of America,

the rich brogue of Ireland, some nasal
English voices—all talking and laughing at once, so loudly.

Miss Magee is laughing musically,
and making fun of Mr. Smiles, who
had been flirting vigorously in the
vaults underneath the Pantheon, and
had proposed to a wrong lady in the
dark.

Mr. Blake sits this evening at my
right hand, and Mrs. Merriman, the
widow, at Mr. Blake's left.

A deaf elderly gentleman sits opposite to me, and is talking out loud
to himself. I hear him muttering,
"Why will that silly old woman,
Mrs. Kingsley, wear a brown wig instead of her own white hair, and why
will she bob her foolish head up and
down, while that idiot Smiles makes
an ass of himself? If that fellow
could only see himself as others see

him he would stop. I hate to see a
man grimacing, gesticulating, and
behaving altogether like his ancestors,
the monkeys." I laugh : but the up-
roar at dinner is so great that nobody
listens to anybody else.

"I like that old boy," remarks Mr.
Blake. "I often go and smoke in
his room. Old Douglas is a chip of
the old block ; he is a great reader, a
traveller ; but, he is as cynical as
Diogenes, and generally rude to his
equals ; but he is fond of animals,
children ; but curiously enough, de-
spises women."

"I suppose Mr. Douglas has had
a disappointment in his youth, poor
man ! I am sorry for him," lisps
Mrs. Merriman with a gentle sigh.

"The devil take her," mutters out
loud Mr. Douglas. "There ! she has
just carried off my favorite bit of

chicken, just the slice I have had my eye upon. What a greedy woman she is, to be sure!"

This ebullition of deaf Mr. Douglas, is intended for Mrs. Melligrew, a fat, ruddy faced Englishwoman, in military mourning, scarlet and black, who is just depositing upon her plate the wing of a chicken, some stuffing, etc., unconscious of Mr. Douglas's remarks.

The dinner is over, and we all go up to the drawing-room.

Olga, Mrs. Blake, and I, go and sit in the balcony, and from that observatory watch the different boarders. Mr. Morris disappears to his den. All the old ladies sit together at one end of the room. The girls cluster round Mr. Smiles and a Mr. Chambers, a mild disciple of Mr. Smiles, who laughs at all his jokes,

and is his shadow. Mr. Smiles is
now in his element, he stalks off to
the piano, and with great *entrain*
sings the famous couplet "L'amour
est un enfant de bohême." All
the young ladies join in this chorus,
even Olga and Mr. Blake chime
in from the balcony. Mr. Smiles
sings this very comically, and with all
the appropriate gestures of an artist.

"Do you see that nice-looking old
lady sitting there?" says Olga,
pointing out an old lady with soft
brown eyes and white hair, "that is
Miss Peleg. If anybody feels at all
poorly—it does not matter about the
symptoms, those are of no con-
sequence—we go to Miss Peleg, and
she gives everybody the same medi-
cine: two teaspoonfuls of Birch's
Salts. A cold in the head, indigestion, neuralgia, rheumatism, etc., etc.,

treated in the same way; for Miss
Peleg believes implicitly in this unfailing remedy and when any of the
boarders feel queer, they go up to
Miss Peleg to be *Birched;* and if
anybody dies, it is because they
have not taken those wonderful salts
in time. Since I am at Madame
Dupont's, I have had Birch's Salts,
at least forty times, and I live!"

Mr. Blake is now called upon to
play. He is very obliging—does not
make a fuss. He plays the "Coulin,"
that grand, pathetic, old Irish air,
and he plays it so exquisitely that he
is made to play it a second, and even
a third time. He then accompanies
Miss Magee, who sings "Kate Kear-
ney," "My Love is like a red, red
Rose," and "The Wearing of the
Green." Olga and I remark that Mrs.
Merriman's smile is no longer child-

like and bland, as she watches the pretty Irish girl sing those wild pathetic airs as only an Irish girl can sing them. Perhaps the widow feels a little jealous as she perceives the admiration that Mr. Blake evidently has for this charming Hibernian, with her sunny smile, her ringing laugh, and musical brogue.

"I am sure that Mr. Blake is a little bit in love with Miss Magee," whispers Olga to me on the balcony; "and I fancy that the widow does not like it. I should like Mr. Blake to marry Mary Magee; they would be so well suited. They are both musical, very Irish, and she is such a bright, unaffected girl. Now Mrs. Merriman is a kind of female Blue Beard—a wolf in sheep's clothing. I should not like her to kill Mr. Blake, for he is a nice little fellow."

" You and Miss Magee are hard upon
this unfortunate widow. I think her
rather attractive ; she has a low sweet
voice ; her manners are good. I con-
fess that this eternal sweet smile, provokes me."

" Now let us retire to our bedroom," says Olga. " We have had a
good dose of gossip and scandal, let us
go before we either of us have said
something that we shall regret pro-
foundly the next morning. I do envy
those quiet people, who never do,
say or write an impulsive thing ; who
never get into scrapes. They may be a
little dull, perhaps, but how safe they
are—how respectable ! "

IV.

OLGA and I now go regularly to
Madame Latour's studio. An old

man with a long white beard, furrowed face, attired in the costume of a monk, is our model. I feel that I make great strides in art, Madame Latour is such a good teacher. She comes into our studio once a-day for about an hour; but her advice is so good, her corrections so conscientious, that the progress we make is remarkable. My study of the monk is the second best; Olga's is the best. She signs those two works, as a proof of her approbation.

Madame Latour allows us now and then to come into her studio and watch her process of working. She is painting a Bacchante: the head thrown back, vine leaves encircling the red-brown hair, and eyes full of voluptuousness and fire; the throat and neck are beautifully modelled, and over the bosom is a gorgeous leopard skin. One hand presses a bunch of grapes, the other hangs listlessly at her side.

At four o'clock the pupils leave the studio. Olga and I usually saunter through the streets of Paris, look into the shops, and often drop into some of the beautiful old Roman Catholic churches. The quiet, the subdued light pouring in through the colored windows, the paintings, the incense, the solemn peals of the organ, the fresh voices of *les enfants du chœur* in their white and colored garments, the harmony of the architecture, is an attraction to the artistic temperament.

One afternoon we had a sort of religious discussion. I said that I found the so-called Low Church cold, unsympathetic, and even very dull; and going to pray at stated hours and days formal and unnatural.

Now, in Catholic communities the churches are always opened; and when you need prayer, and would desire repose, it is a comfort to drop into one of those old churches; and even if no service is going on, it is soothing to listen to the silence, to be in an atmosphere of subdued light. There is more poetry in the Roman Catholic faith, with all its grievous errors.

"I am a pagan," says Olga. "Nature is my god; the sun, the stars, and the yellow moon are my deities. On Sundays I generally take long rambles in the country with Fido, my dog, and my little maid Nina. Sometimes, when the spirit moves me, which is seldom, I go to hear the celebrated *pasteur*, Monsieur Bonchemin, *le pasteur à la mode*. All the ladies run after him,

and that is one of the reasons I go so
seldom to his chapel, for it makes me
ill to see how women turn the heads
of those servants of God! Monsieur
Bonchemin is a man of great eloquence.

" His sermons are great intellect-
ual treats : he never reads his sermons, and that is such an advantage !
His utterance is delightful, voice
beautiful; he never hesitates for a
word. He is very handsome, like a
St. John, with a slightly melancholy
rêveur expression, which is fascinating. His hands are beautiful, and
he knows it, for one of these append-
ages he lets hang gracefully down
the pulpit cushion. He is the
woman's *pasteur*—a kind of Protes-
tant Pope: his power is great, his
appeals to the conscience are search-
ing and keen, and he certainly makes

me feel horribly uncomfortable; but
when I see all those elegant toilettes,
those wonderful Paris bonnets. I
do not feel at all as if I was wor-
shipping an unseen God—merely
listening to a handsome, eloquent
preacher.

"So I prefer nature: I feel more
elevated looking at a fine sunset, or
at the sea, than kneeling upon a hard
footstool, surrounded by silks, satins,
and prosperity. *Vanitas vanitatum,
omnia vanitas!* Do you know Mr.
Morris is a Positivist, a follower of
Comte? He worships humanity.
He tells me he does his duty, and
tries to love his neighbor. As far as
I know, his notion of duty is to paint
pictures, and I do not think he cares
for his neighbors. He is often much
depressed; and really I do not wonder at it, for it is hard to have

11

little in this world, and to think he will have nothing at all in the next."

At this point of the conversation, who should we see but Mr. Morris, in an old battered wide-awake, a very shabby coat, and a portfolio under his arm. Olga taps him on the back with her parasol. He starts, and looks uncomfortable. We tell him that we were just talking about him, and saying that it was a pity he did not believe in a future state.

"The boulevards are scarcely a fit place for a discussion upon the immortality of the soul," answers Mr. Morris smiling; "but if you are anxious to know my belief, all I can say is, that my mind is not made up. I feel that I have a soul, and do not think it will perish."

"Let us leave the soul alone," ex-

claims Olga, looking into a cake shop.
" I shall perish if I do not eat. Let
us enter this *pâtisserie*, and fill our
inner beings ! "

Mr. Morris tries to escape. He
declares that he is not in a fit state
to be seen walking in ladies' society ;
he has been sketching all day at the
Jardin des Plantes.

" You know, Mr. Morris, that I am
also a Bohemian, and do not mind
how shabby you look."

We insist so much that he consents
to remain with us, and so we enter
the shop, devour a number of cream
éclairs, and Olga orders a parcel of
cakes, biscuits, and *bonbons* to be
made up for a small *protégé* of hers,
a cripple boy, whom she is going to
visit the following day.

We walk through the Tuileries
Gardens. How imposing the ruins

of this once mighty palace look in
this twilight!

There is something very grand
about the old Château now, as it
stands there mutilated. What pages
of history have been enacted there!
—a whole past swept away! The
Gardens are at this hour deserted.
The statues seem quite mournful,
and look like ghosts in this dim gray
light. A solitary white swan is
gliding warily in a dismal pond; the
trees make a dark background; the
clouds are purple; there is a thin
mist over everything, and just over
the ruined helpless palace peeps a
young crescent moon. The sentinel
looks like an uneasy spirit, as he
stands at the gate of the Garden.

We cross the bridge, down the
Quai Voltaire, and peep leisurely into all the bric-a-brac shops, and lastly

we enter an old curiosity shop, full
of quaint odd pieces of furniture, old
china, old plate, etc. It is a queer little
den. The shopman is a Jew, named
Solomon—a thin, wiry old fellow,
with a few scanty white hairs brushed
carefully over his narrow head, spec-
tacles falling down his long thin
nose. In his wrinkled hand he holds
a lamp, which casts mysterious
shadows here and there in the small
shop. "A picture for Rembrandt,"
I think, as I watch the old Jew
ferreting out his antique wares,
beautiful bronzes, laces, old books,
prints, etc.

"What a splendid bit of old tapestry! It would look well in my little
studio," exclaims Mr. Morris, "but I
must not be tempted to buy it."

Olga goes up to the shopman,
whispers something mysteriously,

and the piece of tapestry is folded up and presented to Mr. Morris. "A souvenir from me," says Olga to him, "in remembrance of this charming walk."

Mr. Morris changes color, looks bewildered, refuses, but Olga insists, so he naturally ends by gratefully accepting it.

I am presented with a pair of antique gold earrings, which in the innocence of my heart I had admired.

"You see what it is to go out with this Lady Bountiful; one dare not express a wish," says Mr. Morris.

"The pleasure is greater in giving than in receiving, so say nothing more about it."

We meet Uranie at the door of the *pension*, who tells me, to my great amazement, that my cousin, Mr. Horace Dashwood, "a varie prettie boy," is upstairs, waiting to see me.

"How very absurd!" Olga and I both exclaim, and before we can make any further remark my cousin stands before us.

"Glad to see you both," Horace shouts, shaking hands with us heartily; "what wild Bohemians you are to be sure!—meandering about Paris, not coming in to dinner, and not telling anybody where you go."

"I am the culprit," says Mr. Morris, "I really thought it a pity to go indoors such a lovely evening, so I begged the young ladies to dine at a restaurant."

Mr. Morris looks much confused, bids us good-night, and Horace follows us upstairs.

"Who on earth is that fellow? in such a shabby old coat and battered

wide-awake? An artist, of course.
I cannot understand how two fashion-
ably dressed girls could walk out with
a man in such a beggarly costume.
You consider him a genius, innocent
young creatures, simply because he
looks dirty."

"Now, Mr. Dashwood, I will not
allow you to call Mr. Morris dirty;
he is a great artist, and no doubt a
man of genius too. You think, evidently, that the coat makes the man.
Some men do depend entirely upon
their tailor for success in the world;
Mr. Morris is above such a considera-
tion. He has a soul above buttons."

" Well, I wish he had some more
buttons to his coat. I am sorry, Mademoiselle Olga, if I have hurt your feelings. All I can say is, that if artists
are all like Mr. Morris then I would
rather not know any. But let us drop

this very unpleasant topic. You look very cross, Mademoiselle Olga."

Olga pouts, and disappears from the room.

"I suppose I have annoyed her. Is she engaged to that wild Bohemian in the old wide-awake?"

"No, she is not; but he is a very great admirer of hers—in fact, I am sure the man is in love with her. So you ought to be more careful, and not give vent to all your notions about artists. Mr. Morris will one day make his mark in the world."

Horace gives a long contemptuous whistle: "I do not pretend to understand artists; they are a race apart."

After a little talk about family affairs Olga returns. To my amusement she has changed her dress, and put on a most becoming lilac silk dress, and placed a coquettish lilac ribbon in her wavy hair. I, of course, make no outward and visible sign of my astonishment; but evidently this inconsistent little maiden is a flirt, and consequently, bent upon making a conquest of my cousin, the famous woman-hater!

"Won't you and Mr. Horace come into my parlor and have some supper? —but you must not abuse Mr. Morris, or we shall quarrel dreadfully."

An exquisite little supper is laid out on the table. A couple of lamps shed a soft light. The water is hissing in the urn. Comfort, luxury, and artistic objects make this room a little Paradise. The windows are open, and in the balcony stand masses of roses, heliotropes, and lilies of the valley.

"What a lovely room!" exclaims Horace. "Paris taste, good English comfort: what more can a mortal require?"

"Yes, Mr. Dashwood, though I am an artist and a Bohemian, I do like pretty things, and no end of luxury. I hope that you admire my dress? it is made by a very fashionable dress-maker." And she makes him a profound courtesy.

"I have been admiring you; such a toilette could only come out of the hands of a Parisian dressmaker, and those dear little shoes that I spy are works of art."

Olga takes off her slipper, and hands it to Horace for nearer inspection. It is very small, of lilac satin, embroidered with silver braid.

"Cinderella's slipper; and you, Horace, are the Prince," I remark.

"Oh no, Mr. Dashwood is not gallant enough for that: his chief failing

is not to admire us poor women, alas !
But I think we can do without his
admiration. Have some sparkling
moselle or champagne, or both, and
eat same of the *pâté de lièvre*, Mr.
Horace, and tell me what you have
been-doing with your great self since
I had the pleasure of seeing you, more
than a year ago."

"Well, I have been doing what
most of us Englishmen spend the
greater part of our lives in doing,
that is, killing beasts, birds, and fishes,
viz., hunting, shooting, and fishing.
You foreigners can hardly understand or appreciate this mode of life."

"Well, I do think," answers Olga,
"that hunting and shooting is very
cruel sport : to see a number of big,
burly men, spending their energies
running after a poor fox, or a little
hare, it seems wicked ; and as for deer-

stalking, I simply think it is a crime.
I cannot understand how any man
can wound a beautiful deer, with its
splendid horns and lovely piteous
eyes, looking so pleading; no, I think
it cowardly. I do not think fishing
so bad," says Olga. "It is rather
nice sport; one sits in a boat, with a
pretty landscape all about, for the
scenery is generally lovely, the water
delicious, and one has merely to wait
for the fish; and when it is caught
the poor thing does not seem to dis-
like it so very much, he does not
scream or bleed. No, fishing is rather a poetical pastime."

Horace laughs heartily. "You
know little about fishing if you imagine that one has merely to wait
quietly for the fish to be hooked; but
it is no use my trying to initiate you
into the mysteries of fishing in your

drawing-room. When you come over to England we shall have some fishing together, I hope."

"Oh, that will be so jolly! I shall be mad with delight if I can just fish up a salmon." And Olga claps her hands at the mere anticipation of such a triumph.

"We shall not begin by salmon-fishing, I assure you; but I must retire, Mademoiselle Olga. I have much enjoyed my evening here. We shall meet to-morrow at breakfast, for I am staying in this house. So *bon soir.*"

The next morning, at breakfast, Horace sits between Olga and me, to the evident disgust of poor Mr. Morris, who watches us gloomily from his side of the table. Mr. Blake is sitting near Mary Magee, in close confabulation, to the dismay of the widow. Mr. Smiles is between the two young American girls, flirting cleverly with the two. Miss Hutchinson is smiling radiantly upon a redhot Radical. We can overhear a little of their conversation.

"Why should not women be in Parliament? they are more eloquent, more tenacious than men."

"Did you ever hear such rubbish?" says Horace. "If that fellow goes on talking such arrant bosh I shall surely have an indigestion. I hate Radicals; they never look gentlemanly. Now look at this man, his coat does not fit him properly, his nails are black. Now a Conservative always looks a gentleman."

Immediately after breakfast we all three decide upon going to Asnières to see Olga's little *protégé*, the cripple boy.

V.

It is a glorious morning. We got out of the train at Asnières. The river looks so tempting, that we get into a little boat and Horace rows us.

He decidedly looks to great advantage in the boat. He is attired in a well-made suit of light gray cloth; his bright, deep blue eyes are full of fun and honesty; his chest is broad and well-developed; he is the best type of the " muscular " school. We get out of the boat and walk across a field full of wild flowers. We all pick some daisies and buttercups to give to poor little Victor.

" I am afraid that he is not long for this world," says Olga. " I fear

he is slowly pining away.   His mother
died during the siege of Paris, lit-
erally of starvation, for she could
not swallow either horseflesh, rats,
or cats ; so little Victor is living with
his old *grand'mère*.   The little boy
is a cripple, and in a consumption ;
but his father, a most intelligent,
honest workman, will not believe that
his child is seriously ill.   There is
the house, that little white place
amongst the trees; it is a kind of
modest inn, where one can have fish,
or rather *friture*, bread and butter,
and cheap wine.

"All right," shouts Horace ; "I am
hungry.   I shall order all the fish in
the house to be fried ; besides, it will
put some money into those poor
people's pockets."

The old *grand'mere* is standing at
the door of the small inn ; a fine type

12

of old age. Her hair is snowy white,
a colored *fichu* is pinned across her
broad chest ; by her side totters a pale,
thin, emaciated little boy, so transparent looking, that one could almost
fancy a strong breath of wind would
waft him away, holding to his *grand'-
mère's* skirts. On seeing Olga a
bright sunny smile illuminates his
wan, white face.

" He has been inquiring after you,
mademoiselle," says the *grand'mère*,
" *n'est-ce pas,* Victor? You are glad
to see Mademoiselle Olga ? "

The child creeps to her, and Olga
gives him some toys, cakes, and *bonbons.*

Horace takes him on his knees, and
gives him a box of soldiers ; the child
at first seems a little frightened, but
my cousin soon makes friends with
him, and they chatter quite gayly to-

gether. *La mère* Gigun looks sadly at her delicate grandchild, and tells us with a big sigh that he is getting weaker and weaker.

"What a lovely face he has!—such long, soft brown, curly hair, large hazel eyes, with such a wistful expression in them. How I should like to have a good picture of him!" mutters *mère* Gigun, "for no photograph can do justice to him."

"That is an idea! Let us come and paint him," says Olga.

"I will do his portrait and give it to you and his father; but you must allow my friend, Miss Larcom, to paint you and the child also. She wants a *sujet* for a picture."

"Only too happy to think that my old face can be of use. I am quite at your *disposition*, mademoiselle."

I thank the old woman. We ar-

range to come the following day with
our easels, canvases, and paint-boxes.
Before leaving we order some fried
goujons for our lunch.   Horace com-
pliments the old woman upon her
cookery, and insists upon her accepting a twenty-franc piece, in order
that she may get a few delicacies for
the child.

Before leaving, Olga takes Victor
upon her knee and tells him a story.
That is his greatest treat ; for he is
an imaginative child, and likes to
hear about fairies, imps, elves, etc.
Victor exists in a kind of Wonderland,
and firmly believes that he is always
surrounded by fairies.   His *grand'-*
mère tells us that he often says he
will be glad to go and live among the
fairies : that is his notion of death ; a
change from what he is now to a beautiful being who lives among flowers,

feeds upon honey and fruits, has wings, and visits the stars.

*   *   *   *

Upon returning to the boarding-house that evening we find our invitations from Madame Latour; it is for the promised fancy ball to take place that day fortnight.

No one can make up their minds as to who or what he or she will personate.

Olga first thinks of going as a star, next as a dryad, or as a sea-nymph.

"Do go as an Ophelia," suggests Mr. Morris.

" Oh, I should have to look melancholy all the evening! A lively Ophelia would be so absurd."

" You would be an ideal Ophelia," continues Mr. Morris. "You have just the right hair, the eyes, the figure, and the expression."

" The crazy look in the eyes," barks out Horace. " Do take my advice, Mademoiselle Olga, and go in a costume that suits your general mood and disposition."

" Happy thought!" exclaims Olga. " I shall go as a *diavolina*—an imp from the regions downstairs."

" That's right. Hurrah!" shouts Horace; "and I shall attend the ball as his infernal majesty himself, with a long tail, horns, and a pitchfork."

" *Convenus*," laughs Olga.

Mr. Morris looks pale and very cross, and scowls furiously at my cousin, who screams out:

" Louisa, you might as well dress as an Ophelia; only your fat, red cheeks and tendency to *embonpoint* might be a little incongruous."

" You are very rude! I mean to go as a *vivandière des zouaves.* In a blue vest, scarlet knickerbockers, white waistcoat. a gold *képi* on my head, and a little barrel filled with cognac at my side."

" Delightful idea. We shall all have a drop now and then to revive our drooping spirits."

" Now, Mr. Morris, how will you dress? I particularly wish you to look to advantage," says Olga, going up to him. Let me think what would suit your character as an artist. a poet. a philosopher." (Olga darts a saucy look at Horace, who is studying pertinaciously the pattern of the carpet.) " I have it. You must go as Hamlet in the ' Inky cloak.' I order you. Mr. Morris. Now, will you? won't you obey me?"

" I should have gladly gone as

Hamlet if you had consented to be
Ophelia," whispers Mr. Morris.

"Oh, that would have been too
remarkable! Besides which, I should
very likely be in wild spirits, and that
would not do for Ophelia. No, go as
Hamlet, and I shall dance the first
dance with you."

Mr. Morris promises, and bidding
us good-night, disappears to his den
upstairs.

"I do not like that man," growls
out my cousin, the moment the door
closes upon Mr. Morris; "he is so
unhealthy in all his views and notions
of life. That artist nature seems unnatural to me. It would do Mr.
Morris a vast deal of good to hunt,
shoot, and fish. It would make him
manly; his notions of everything are
sickly, false, and absurd."

"Well, Mr. Dashwood, I am sur-

prised at your disobedience!" exclaims Olga, standing up and flushing
with excitement. "I did tell you
several times that nothing can annoy
me more than to hear Mr. Morris
abused. Your idea of life is sport.
All right. Mr. Morris loves art; he
is a great artist and musician. He
might dress better, but it is not
affectation on his part; simply he does
not care about the cut of his coat nor
about the particular shade of his neck-
tie, etc. Mr. Morris will, I am sure,
be a great man one of these days.
Meanwhile, let him alone, or we shall
quarrel seriously. You are a naughty
boy; the more you abuse Mr. Morris
the more I shall like him."

"Well, I shall not mention Mr.
Morris's name again."

When Horace is gone, I ask Olga if
she thinks that my cousin is improved.

"I have not thought much about him, one way or the other." ('What a story!' I inwardly ejaculate.) "He has good qualities, but he is fearfully prejudiced. He is a type of the modern young man; no feeling for Art, but fond of sport. He is generous and manly."

"I wonder if he will ever fall·in love?"—saying this I peep slyly at Olga through the corners of my eyes.

She colors up. "I do not think that it is in him to care much for any one."

"Well, I think you are mistaken, and I sometimes think that he does actually care for some young lady."

"Really? Oh! do tell me all about it: he is your cousin, so it is natural that I should take some interest in him."

" Ask no questions and I shall tell you no stories. I cannot say anything for certain, it is a supposition on my part. I should like Horace to marry; he would make a first-rate husband."

" Have you seen the girl you think he is in love with?"

" I have seen her, she is a great friend of mine." And I look hard at Olga, who pretends not to understand, gets very red, rushes off to the piano and plays deliciously a valse of Chopin.

The next morning Olga and I go to Asnières. We have our easels, canvases and painting materials. When we reach the quiet inn, we perceive *mère* Gigun at the door, looking very dismal; the child is sleeping.

" I am afraid that before next month

he will be lying by his poor mother's grave, in the little *cimetière* over there, he is ebbing away."

We both go up to the bedroom. In a small white bed lies the child, a feverish spot on each cheek : he opens his big eyes and smiles a welcome.

" We are come to paint your picture," Olga says, kissing him. " Here are some flowers for you."

Victor brightens up, he is propped by pillows. The old *grand'mère* sits close to him, the window is open, and an acacia tree in full bloom casts a delicious fragrance ; a cage with two canaries stands on the sill.

I sketch the room as it is ; the sick child sitting up playing with the flowers, the *grand'mère* with her wrinkled face and sweet, sad gray eyes and snowy hair, making such a contrast to the spiritual, unearthly face of the wee

grandson. The old woman knits a
brown woollen stocking, and a tear
now and then drops on her hands as
she looks at the child.

Olga, while painting, tells Victor
a story of a little boy who was carried
away by the fairies, and is still living
with them in a beautiful blue palace
up in the clouds ; he is the only little
boy there, the fairies are very fond of
of him, pet him much, so he is quite
happy.

Victor's expression gets more and
more ideal and Olga's portrait is growing wonderfully like.

" What a treasure it will be to us ! "
exclaims the old woman. " We shall
prize it, oh so much, mademoiselle ! "

" Why do you look so *triste, grand'-
mère ?* Suppose the fairies take me
away up in their blue palace, you, papa,
and mademoiselle must come also."

A tap at the door; a fine stalwart *ouvrier* in a blue blouse comes in; his face is sunburnt, but very handsome. He bows respectfully to us, hopes that he does not disturb us, and going up to Victor kisses him.

" How are you, *mon fils?* "

" Better, *petit père.* Look at the pictures the ladies are painting of me."

" With your permission, mademoiselle," and he looks at Olga's work. " It is a very good likeness; the expression is perhaps a little more sad, *mais c'est bien lui!* The eyes are perfect, just the color and the expression."

Then he comes round to look at mine.

"Ah, that will make a capital picture, old age and childhood. I compliment you upon your artistic talent."

" Is he not a type of the best kind of French workman ? so intelligent, refined, and so artistic ? " whispers Olga to me. " Well, how are you getting on, Monsieur Lenoir ? " she continues, addressing the *ouvrier*.

" Pretty well, mademoiselle, the *commerce* is just beginning to get on, and we must work hard."

" I do admire the French workman so much ! " says Olga. " Lenoir is not an exception ; no, as a rule, the *ouvriers* are honest, intelligent, and refined ; such a contrast, so superior to those horrid little men one meets on the boulevards, sipping *café*, absinthe, and *eau de vie*."

But it is now getting too dark to work, so kissing Victor, we go down stairs and have a quiet little dinner in the garden.

VI.

A FEW evenings after this sad visit Horace comes into my room, looking rather meek, and, indeed, sheepish.

"I know," he says, "that you are going to laugh at me. Can you guess what I have done?" and he stares uncomfortably out of the window.

"Well, I think I can guess," I reply laughing.

"Oh yes! you can laugh. Go on. Well, what is it?"

"Why, you silly old boy, you have of course fallen head over ears in love with that little sprite, Olga, .. though she is a Bohemian, a Radical, an artist, independent; in fact, the very contrary of what you pretend to admire."

"Well, you have found me out!" and he colors up very much; "but the wonder of wonders is, that she cares a little for me, also, and has consented to become my wife!"

"Nothing surprises me, she is such an inconsistent little damsel. She declared to me not many weeks ago that she would never marry; but I am so glad that she has so soon changed her mind. You are to be congratulated, for she is a charming girl, though she is fond of art, and a Radical."

"It was at the funeral of poor little Victor that I decided upon proposing to her. A look she gave me, a general something in her demeanor that morning, made me feel that I was not indifferent to her; and Olga

13

tells me that my kindness to the child made her care for me against her will."

So the poor little fellow was the unconscious means of making up a match.

I rush off to Olga's room. I find her lying full length upon the hearth-rug; her cheeks are very flushed and her eyes sparkling.

On seeing me she throws a hand-kerchief over her face, saying, " What will you think of me, Louise? I am really ashamed, and cry peccavi; but I really feel so happy. I did not think it possible for me ever to care for any one again, and I now find that I never really loved either number one or number two. I have told your cousin all about those previous affairs; he is such a good fellow, he does not mind at all. Don't laugh at me too much, I am sure you must think me a very odd girl."

" Indeed I do ; that is your charm —so unlike everybody else. But I congratulate you, you and Horace will be very happy together."

" I shall leave the boarding-house as soon as I have packed up all my pretty things, and have them all sent to London."

" You will come and stay at our house till the wedding ? "

" Just what I should like. I have no home, no relatives, no one in the world. Horace will now be everything to me."

* * *

THE fancy ball at Madame Latour's studio is a great success. It is a picnic ball ; the ladies send the eatables, the men the wines. Olga and

I sent a tremendous *pâté de foie gras* and a boar's head.

The *atelier* looks quite grand, brilliantly illuminated and festooned with flowers and evergreens, and a long table laden with all the delicacies of the season. Olga is the belle of the ball, as a *diavolina* in scarlet, gold, and black skirts; little gold horns in her hair, a pitchfork in her hand, and black and red flames worked into the patterns of her dress.

Horace changed his mind, and disguised himself as a wolf. His tail was constantly trodden upon, and then he would roar lustily, to the great amusement of everybody. He and Olga were in high spirits. Naturally, poor Mr. Morris, having heard of their engagement (such secrets always get known), did not appear at the ball; a sure sign that he really cared for Olga.

Mr. Blake is disguised as an orange-tree, Miss Magee as a shepherdess. It is noticed by many that she rests continually under that particular tree, and that the tree hovers continually over her.

My costume of *vivandière* is a great success. One particular gentleman, whose name I shall not divulge, drank more cognac out of my barrel than was good for him.

Madame Latour looks very fine as Queen of the Night, all in black tulle, with silver stars, a crescent moon in her dark hair, and a stuffed owl perched upon her shoulder.

"Well, Olga, so you are going to give up art for matrimony? I am grieved to hear this piece of news; you cannot serve two masters. You will fail."

" Yes, madame, I shall paint more than ever. I do not see why a woman should become a nonentity when she marries. I shall have a studio in our town-house; besides we shall be six months every year on the Continent."

" We shall see," growls Madame Latour. " Do not believe the promises made before marriage. Tell me what Mr. Dashwood says after the ceremony is over. No, I am disappointed; you ought not to have promised me to give yourself entirely to art, and then, when a handsome young fellow comes over here, you give up everything for him. *Violà les femmes !*—no tenacity, no decision of character, no strong will."

" I am catching it," whispers Olga to me; " but it is no use my trying to persuade Madame that I shall paint pictures after my marriage ; but I *will*, and very likely I shall make Horace study art."

A few days after the ball, Horace departs, Uranie calling him a " varrie naughtie boy." He feels he deserves the reproach ; he gives Uraine twenty francs to pacify her, and tells her that she must not abuse him when he is gone.

Mr. Morris leaves the *pension* without bidding Olga or me good-bye. There is a report that he is engaged to be married to the wily widow, who has been making herself strong in Art, and copying at the Louvre.

Mr. Blake goes to Cork to visit his family ; it is rather a curious co-incidence that Miss Magee and her mother should be going over to Erin at that particular time. Miss Hutchinson has gone to New York to study the institutions of the mighty republic. Olga and I, with great regret, bid adieu to Madame Dupont, and all the inmates of the *pension*.

We leave on a sultry morning at the end of June. Uranie has tears in her eyes as she bids us adieu, and declares that we really are " varrie naughtie " to leave. When we reach the station we do not find either Mr. Morris or Mr. Blake awaiting us ; and it is with mixed feelings of pleasure and pain that Olga and I leave bright, beautiful Paris for dreary London ; but Olga declares, with a blush, that it will no longer be dismal, but delightful.